PRAISE FOR
J. WEINTRAUB

I0609849

"J. Weintraub is a connoisseur of the human soul and the thousand shadows residing there. His stories—quiet, introspective, yet with sharp edges—dig to the bottom, reaching down to the nerves of readers and dragging them into a confrontation with the metaphysical twilight of heart and mind. Truly a storyteller at the highest level."

~ Nicola Lombardi,
author of *The Gypsy Spiders and Other Tales of Italian Horror*

"This is such a beautiful, beautiful piece and I absolutely loved it! The ending is profound in its abject simplicity and this will be a proud addition to our anthology!"

~ On "Jenn's Gift" from Jay Chakravarti,
editor of *Cosmic Contact: Science Fiction & Fantasy of First Contact Stories*

A VISIT
TO THE
CATACOMBS

BY
J. WEINTRAUB

From
Dark Owl Publishing, LLC

Arizona

Cover design by Dark Owl Publishing

Visit us on our website at:
www.darkowlpublishing.com

ALSO FROM
DARK OWL PUBLISHING

Collections

The Dark Walk Forward
Baby Monster
John S. McFarland

The Last Star Warden:
Volumes I and II
The Phantom World
The Crimson Star Saga
Episodes
Jason J. McCuiston

The Brotherhood of Secret Darkness and Other Cults, Cabals, and Conspiracies
Jason J. McCuiston

The Tension of a Coming Storm
Adrian Ludens

The Nightmare Cycle
Lawrence Dagstine

The Art of Ghost Writing
Alistair Rey

Bad Dreams and Reflections
Trevor Kennedy

Welcome to Scar Ridge
Jonathon Mast

The Satchel and Other Terrors
The Potion and Other Perilous Libations
Matias Travieso-Diaz

Of Dark Places
Gustavo Bondoni

Vanther the Vanquisher: Bloodquest
Scott Harper

Anthologies
Something Wicked This Way Rides

Novels
The Black Garden
The Mother of Centuries, the sequel to *The Black Garden*
John S. McFarland

The Wicked Twisted Road
D.S. Hamilton

TABLE OF CONTENTS

A VISIT TO THE CATACOMBS

elcome to the catacombs of via Altamontivecchi, the grandest and one of the most ancient in the world. I will be your guide for this special pilgrim's tour in the English language. If you have booked in advance, you will find the number 34 stamped on your ticket. If you have not booked in advance, you have no business being here. Please return tomorrow in the morning when there will be more tours for you in several languages.

For those of you who have booked in advance, please step inside.

Again, welcome to our tour. I trust you have all signed the waiver and have also had the opportunity to visit the facilities as instructed? Good. The visit will be of a long duration, and there will be no opportunities once we are inside. Now, please hand over your tickets. Twelve places only. Thank you. Thank you. Please step inside. Thank you.

Before we proceed further, several cautions need to be spoken. Please stay together and close to me so you will hear all my instructions and absorb all the history and the other observations without the need for repetitions. But more important, you must not stray from the group. This is absolute. The galleries of via Altamontivecchi are quite intricate and are estimated to extend over 15 kilometers, longer than even the great complex of Domitilla outside the walls of Rome. Galleries lead into galleries in a most confusing manner, intersect with upper and lower levels, and at its outermost extremities to the east and to the south merge with unsafe pagan columbria linked to the worship of Mithra and Sabazius. If you become lost in these extremities, there is no assurance you will find your way out or be found. In the past century, in fact, an entire class, sixteen students and their professor, disappeared without a trace.

Of course, you might be saying to yourself, "All I need do is to follow my way back towards the light!" But that is not such an easy thing as you might think. I myself, once thought in a similar manner, but I mistakenly took a passage that led me in the opposite direction, and when I tried to retrace my steps, I could only see an occasional flickering, like fireflies on a moonless night. Fortunately, I had not penetrated far, but there are sectors where huge crevices have opened, quite deep enough to swallow anyone who has strayed from the guided tour and then gone from there into eternity. Even in ancient days, when the galleries were new and expanding, guides like me were hired and passages were obstructed to prevent visitors and relatives from losing their way and eventually polluting these holy places with their unsanctified corpses.

So, please stay with the group and avoid curious wanderings. We want you to enjoy your visit!

Also, please avoid touching the walls and masonry. The galleries we will be visiting are quite safe, but catacombs require a soft, penetrable rock like this tufa. Slabs can be easily dislodged, and there are pockets just beneath the surface where the rock becomes loose and granular, almost like a liquid. Also, the ancients strengthened many of the vaults and stress points with brick, mortar, and plaster, all subject to erosion. You do not want to risk bringing down several tons of volcanic rock upon our heads for a souvenir.

And yes, to remove anything from the premises, from the smallest stone to an undiscovered fragment of a relic, is a criminal offense. The Altamontivecchi catacombs are a national treasure.

So, we are understood? Are there questions? Good. We can begin our tour. Please hold onto the railing and proceed carefully. The descent is steep, and the steps are as old as the catacombs themselves, carved directly from the rock and rubbed smooth by the footsteps of numberless pilgrims just like yourself. Note the small square apertures cut into the walls where oil lamps were placed to light the way for many centuries, depositing an impressive residue of soot and grime along the passageway. Another reason to avoid contact with the walls and to thank providence for the miracle of electricity.

We arrive now at the most recent construction, an extensive marble altar erected shortly after the rediscovery of the catacombs during the so-called Bloody Schism. Here it is said that many sacraments were performed in private until the authorities of the Counter Reformation put a stop to it. Note the fine decorative ornament on the altar stone, with garlands and cornucopia almost pagan in their exuberance.

Now as we turn down this path... and then into this one, you will note that all natural light has vanished behind us. Without the electric lights on the walls and the torch in my hand, we would be in total darkness. Here, along both walls, in the displays behind the glass, are the artifacts that have been found in the tombs and their surrounding spaces. Note the iron, bronze, and ceramic lamps that I mentioned earlier. Also, we have the digging tools—mattocks and picks—left by the *fossores*, numerous offerings—coins, glass vials, earthenware vessels—and mementoes of the dead: rings, bracelets, and brooches, and even this toy doll, carved from ivory, found embedded in the stucco sealing the grave of the eight-year-old Aurelia Hyacinth.

In the far corner, you see pottery shards, cooking pots, stone fetishes, and iron utensils of great antiquity. These were found at the end of the last century with the collapse of a wall during an excavation that revealed behind it a cavern hidden since Neolithic times. Among the shards and cookware were fragments of human bones, also scorched like the pottery. It is unknown whether this was the result of primitive funerary practices, or, as one radical archaeologist suggests, signs of ritual cannibalism among our native ancestors. In either case, it speaks of the long habitation of the site and its ancient ceremonial significance.

Now, as we turn into the central gallery, look up to the roof of the vault. Near what was once a skylight, you see the great image of the *Majestas Domini*, thought to have been painted in the late third century. Scholars tell us that since this is the first known portrayal of Christ Enthroned surrounded by a nimbus—a device typical of pagan iconography—the painting is likely to have been superimposed upon an earlier fresco of Helios, God of the Sun.

It is also exactly here at this spot, just where that young lady is standing—no, no, miss, you don't need to move—where Tomas the shepherd fell through that very skylight above us to his death. The opening had been sealed long before to prevent such an unfortunate incident, but perhaps several months of floods and the seepage led to its collapse. We can only hope that enough natural light followed from his fall to illuminate the magnificent image above him as Tomas lay there on his broken back, dying.

Tomas was given credit for the rediscovery of the Altamontivecchi catacombs, but in truth, it was his herd of abandoned sheep and his barking dog that brought the villagers to the site. And if it had not been for the intercession of Father Adrian, now beatified by the Holy See, the opening may have been quickly resealed by the superstitious peasants and the catacombs again forgotten. A simple parish priest, Father Adrian was also a learned man and deeply committed to the defense of the Church against a violent iconoclasm then wreaking havoc and bloodshed across the countryside. What a superb witness then is this striking vision above us to the importance and power of the image for the first believers, the founders of the true Church.

As we descend deeper into the earliest parts of the complex and turn here, we arrive at the Corridor of the Martyrs, the most important of our pilgrim sites. Yes, it is quite impressive, isn't it? Row upon row, tier upon tier of burial slots, graves like shelves or berths on a ship carved into the rock. They are called *loculi* and they extend seemingly endlessly into the darkness, ample evidence of the ferocity of the third- and fourth-century persecutions, particularly during the reigns of Valerian and Diocletian.

No, all the *loculi* here were emptied of their remains long ago, some the victims of barbarian plundering, others translocated to the surface where they could be venerated more publicly, and still others transported far beyond our borders during the eighth and ninth centuries when the market for relics was especially active and profitable.

And, of course, not all of these are the graves of martyrs or saints. Most of the epitaphs and graffiti were inscribed years after the burials, and entire communities wished to be entombed near those who could intercede on their behalf in the world to come. But note the simplicity and starkness of the arrangement and the lack of ornament or display, testimony to the modest circumstances of the original believers, but also the willingness of those in higher stations to humble themselves as part of a congregation before God.

But still, martyrs and saints were laid to rest here, and we know for a fact that in this tiny niche the holy Palladian once reposed, and in these six graves, one atop the other, lay the six Coronati—Praetorian guards converted, brutally tortured, and thereafter crowned with the gift of martyrdom. Here, at my eye level, was once the saintly Petros, and in this narrow slot just below lay his skin, now venerated in Budapest. In here the holy Valeria was interred, although her head was claimed for via Altamarina. Here Palomon the

Elder, and by his side Palomon the Younger, or at least those parts that could be retrieved from the horses. Posidius. Pontesilea, Aprius—said to be a follower of the anti-Pope Novatian—Dalmatius, Onager, Vitalia, Rubilla, Viktor, and the one, two, three, four, five sons of Renata, and above, the blessed Renata herself. Beneath this cavity, you can still see engraved the single word *Stercorius*, or "abandoned in garbage," although whether this is the name of the martyr or simply where his remains were first deposited is unknown.

These two cavities, when opened, first seemed empty, but the inscriptions and the traces of paint seemingly depicting flames on the arcosolium of this one convinced the ecclesiastical authorities that the heavy residue of ash found inside was none other than St. Eventius. In the other one? Nothing more than two pairs of pincers were found, but it was believed that the shreds of flesh soldered into the grooves of the prongs once belonged to St. Marcella.

Farther on down, the *loculi* become sparser, but the graves increase again in number as we move into the latter half of the fourth century with its multitude of heterodoxies, and then at the end of the passageway, behind the grating, the surprisingly ornate ossuarium of the Heresiarch Ostian, who was interred here with the bones of two hundred of his slaughtered followers. If you visit the smaller complex at via Altamarina, you will see the crypticum of the Archbishop Fabian, who has been credited with the extermination of the cult.

Now, allow me to turn on the interior light, and as you pass the grating, look toward the lunettes of the arcosolium just above the altar, and you will see a series of remarkably realistic chthonic and zoomorphic representations painted by an anonymous Thracian artist, who, if the inscription is to be believed, was sympathetic to the sect and eventually joined them here.

Oh, my... oh, no... Don't be frightened. Please, madam... This happens on occasion. Power failures like these are common in the late summer. Or perhaps there's been a short circuit. The severe humidity. Here, let me try something. This switch just over here... Sometimes after an overload, we can simply click it off—there— and then wait a moment before I click it back on... There... No, that's not it. I suppose it is a power failure. We have had a very oppressive summer, and I'm sure the lights, air conditioners, refrigerators, and such above ground are all in the black, too, just like here below. But still, we must proceed, and thankfully, I have the light of my torch to guide us. The batteries were replaced several weeks ago, so we should be just fine. But please, stay close to me as we move on.

These stairs will lead us to the next level below and into the fifth century. I will shine the light on the steps but be sure to take hold of the railing as you descend. Yes, I know it is a bit unsteady from the porous nature of the rock here, but it will be perfectly safe if you proceed carefully… Here, I have reached bottom, and if you will first gather around me, we will continue into the gallery.

On this level, we witness the enormous growth of what was once a tiny congregation of true believers now spread across the land despite the state's attempts to eradicate them. Again, row upon row, tier upon tier of graves, excavated at considerable cost, yet worth the expense to those who wished to be interred near the saints and martyrs of previous generations.

Here much of the original plaster and terracotta tiles are still in place, along with the remains interred inside. Apparently, this level was unknown to the barbarians and others who vandalized the tombs. But they would not have found much of value had they in fact penetrated this far. These were ordinary folk, their bones not worthy of public veneration, the mementoes interred with them—copper jewelry, vials of unguents, small coins, and toys for the children—all of little artistic or monetary worth. But still, a unique site since many of the epitaphs are as visible as when they were inscribed into the plaster. See HIC REQUIESCIT here, and here HIC REQUIESCIT, and here HIC REQUIESCIT, and up and down the gallery HIC REQUIESCIT, HIC REQUIESCIT, HIC REQUI-ESCIT. Not very creative, these ordinary folk, but an impressive display, nevertheless.

As we turn towards the chamber reserved for your group, the corridor becomes very narrow. Please, single file here, and you might want to place your hands on the shoulders of the person in front of you until we reach the great Cryptoporticus of Danilo at the *Spelunca Magna*.

Now attention, please, as we turn here. The rubble you see on your right spilling into your path seals a transverse gallery that once led to the famous Capella of the Good Shepherd—all destroyed when the passage and several others collapsed five years ago last month during the previous eruption of Altamontivecchi and the ensuing earthquake. An unredeemable loss. By the by, I hope you have had the opportunity to visit our Altamontivecchi volcano during the evening time. A spectacular display, particularly around the crater where the lava flow is especially impressive.

Here you see the plaque recently dedicated to the Dacian pilgrims who were awaiting the return of their guide when the first tremors struck. Unfortunately, my good friend Nicolo, who was still on the surface, was killed instantly in the collapse of the basilica, and with so much chaos and devastation above, little thought was given to those awaiting Nicolo here below. Of course, it probably was no matter, since the galleries and cubiculi hereabouts seemed to have disappeared completely. At least, when shafts were sunk from above, they struck nothing but rock, and excavations here were abandoned in face of the tons of solid granite that had tumbled into the passageway.

It was no accident, some superstitious people say, that the incident occurred in the vicinity of the Cubiculum of Danilo, and here we are. Note the brick masonry on the vault, required to support the tufa in this sector, and the plaster surfaces where fragments of color from the frescoes that once appeared here can still be seen. Over there, behind the grating, is the throne of Danilo carved from solid rock and where bits of gold leaf still sparkle in the light of my torch.

On either side are the seats occupied by the catechist and presiding deacon, and the low stone benches were probably set aside for the instruction of the catechumens. No one knows what rites were performed here, although there are suggestions of a corrupt Eucharist liturgy. The paintings were largely destroyed during the purifications of the late fifth century but note the remnants of la banquet scene on the vault, either a celestial or diabolical convivium, and over there is what might be the earliest representation of the devil. You can barely see the gaping mouth of the demon amidst the roaring flames of hell, although some scholars say it is rather the maw of the leviathan about to swallow Jonas and the flames are merely waves.

Behind the throne is the crypt where the sarcophagus of Danilo was to rest. The walls here, too, were once covered with frescoes and grotesqueries, but in this instance even the plaster was scraped from the masonry, and nothing remains. Of course, the great Apostate was never interred here, his ashes scattered to the four winds, but it is said by superstitious people that his spirit animates these corridors when the sun disappears in the west.

Now we descend in this direction, and please form again into a very narrow single line. Careful. The ground is uneven, and you will notice a trembling at your feet as we cross over a very swift subterranean river. The current is especially strong this year because of the heavy summer rains, and this explains the thick moisture on the walls and the chill in the air. No, no, madam, that was only a cold draft, I'm sure, that passed over your feet. From the river, probably. There are no vermin down here.

And here we arrive at our terminus. This chamber is called the Capella of Peace, from the inscription IN PACE AETERNA engraved over the portal.

All of you come inside. You must now remove the robes from your packs and put them on. There are additional robes on the shelf there if you neglected to bring one. Place your packs, your guidebooks, and your other belongings in the corner here. They will be safe.

Be sure all your garments are well covered. The *loculi* here are clean—all remains and offerings, of course, have been removed—but dust and dirt continue to erode from the walls. Use the hoods to protect your heads, but careful not to wrap it around your nose or mouth. It will be close enough for you inside as is.

All the *loculi* here are about the same size, but the elderly among you may want to choose the ones closest to the ground. There are stepladders about for those of you who can climb to a higher tier and are not uncomfortable with the sensation of height.

No, I'm sorry. You must all find a place for yourself. Yes, I know, people do change their minds, but there is nothing I can do about it now. You have come this far, and you must carry on to the end. No, I cannot take anyone back under any circumstances. You must find your place here. There are no benches or resting spots nearby, and besides, you must not leave the chamber in my absence, especially now that we are suffering through a power failure. I assure you that this is an experience that will change you forever. To meditate among our ancient martyrs and saints in this famed *locus sanctus*, to join spiritually a community of primitive believers and the pilgrims and people of God who followed in their path and acted as you are about to act, this is a privilege permitted only to a few, and many have waited in vain for years to participate. As the graffito over there reminds us: *Intra limina sanctorum, quod multi cupiunt et rari accipiunt.*

So, take my hand, and you can slide in right here. That's right, on your back with your arms crossed over your chest. A nice fit. Yes, I know it feels tight. It often feels tight. Our ancestors were smaller than we are, and they usually arrived here in a state of considerable desiccation. But this will help you to remain still. You must not move or shift your position. You certainly do not want to wedge yourself inside, by trying, say, to turn onto your stomach, and be sure, all of you, to avoid sudden movements. Tufa is soft rock, but it is rock nevertheless, and the mattocks have left sharp ridges.

Those tremors? I am sure they are no more than the vibrations from the river running beneath us nearby.

Now, all of you, now that you have found your places and are comfortable, breathe slowly and quietly. If you become anxious, concentrate on breathing more slowly, regularly, silently—otherwise, you will feel as if you are suffocating, which only contributes to your anxiety. Respect the meditations of those around you and the sanctity of the place. Yes, I know. I have participated in this very chamber twice myself. I know how tight it can feel, and I, too, have tasted in my mouth the dirt and the grit of the place. But that is all part of the experience we promised you, as is this... There. I have extinguished my torch, and you find yourself within a darkness so profound it is palpable. Do not be afraid. Study the darkness. Look into the darkness until it becomes one with you and you are one with it, separate from every living thing in the world above.

I can find my way out in the darkness. Ignore the quiet breath of your neighbors and allow the silence to envelop you as I leave.

I should be back before very long.

ROACH

The house, Mark told me, was not far from where Bobby Franks had lived some fifty years before, and even closer to the spot where he had been abducted and, shortly thereafter, brutally murdered. Not that it really mattered, since I was a resident there for less than a day, although it was the first thing Mark wanted to tell me about the house we both then assumed was going to be my home for the next year, and perhaps even longer.

Like many of the free-standing family dwellings built in that neighborhood at the turn of the previous century, it was set back on a small lot, a narrow strip of lawn separating it from the street. It stood on a brick and stone foundation, but its frame was wooden, and its sides were of weathered clapboard that rose up two stories to the pitched, overhanging roof, forming a gable at the front. Many of the roof's slate shingles were of irregular shades, as if there had been frequent replacements; on one side was a vestigial cupola balanced on the other by a brick chimney rising just above it, and I wondered, as we momentarily stood there examining the structure, if the chimney led downward to a working fireplace in the living room.

Dominating the façade was a single-story, wraparound porch, supported by columns and decorated with pediments and spindle work, and although its size was impressive and inviting—I could envision myself whiling away summer afternoons in its shade, a book on my lap and a beer in hand—its paint was chipped and peeling, as it was on the rest of the house, as if it were an enormous cold-blooded creature about to shed its skin.

A narrow alleyway separated the building from the brick walkup apartments on its west side, the kind constructed a generation later as the more affluent families began to abandon the neighborhood for elsewhere. A vacant lot—which probably once held a similar family home—was on its other side, and adjacent to that and probably built around the same time stood another version of the house in front of us. This one, however, had bay windows jutting out from both sides and a pair of domed turrets accompanying the chimney on the roof. Also built on a stone foundation, it, too, was constructed primarily of wood and featured an almost identical veranda. But here there were no peeling surfaces or obvious patchwork, and, in fact, a recent coat of paint, all white, made it seem almost resplendent in the late morning sun. The FOR SALE sign at the edge of its small lawn explained, at least for me, the freshness of its exterior.

"The porch is my favorite part," said Mark, leading me down the short path toward the graying veranda. The floorboards creaked as we walked up its steps. "What do you think of it so far?"

"It's got loads of character," I said, and then added, as I peeled a strip of limp paint off one of its Corinthian columns, "although it does seem a bit rundown."

"I'll admit," said Mark, "the owner hasn't put much into it lately. She's been renting it out for years to students, and you know how that goes. But it'll grow on you, I'm sure, and it's still a pretty good deal in a tight market. But come on inside. I'll show you your room and introduce you to Leonard."

Mark had been my roommate the previous year at the graduate dorm, but when his lab partner, Dave, told him that there was an opening off-campus in Kenwood, he had jumped at the opportunity. Now, almost eight months later, after one of his current roommates had dropped out of school and left, he had given me a call. I still had a couple of months remaining on my current dorm contract, but the prospect of inexpensive private lodging for the summer and perhaps for the next few years as I completed my research and dissertation was inviting. I agreed to spend the night and move in during the upcoming weekend if I liked the place, which Mark was sure I would.

The screen door rattled and squeaked as he pulled it open, but I guess that was to be expected.

"Dan's in the lab," said Mark as we turned from the short entryway into the living room, "but you already know him pretty well. So, say hello to Leonard here."

Leonard was settled deep between two cushions in the dilapidated couch at the center of the room. His knees were almost to his chin, helping to support the massive volume balanced on his thighs. Leonard was studying to be an Egyptologist, and although I could see nothing of his book's contents, gilded scarabs were incised up and down the edges of the otherwise empty cloth binding, and I assumed it to be full of hieroglyphics and diagrams of archaeological digs. The TV across from him was on—broadcasting a black-and-white thriller or detective tale from the forties—but the sound had been turned off, and Leonard, after acknowledging my greeting, returned immediately to his book.

"The furniture's not much," said Mark as we reached the stairs to the second floor and climbed up. "The house is rented unfurnished, and the tables, chairs, and stuff have been accumulated over the years from yard sales, back alleys, and the like. But the beds are comfortable, and there's plenty of closet and book space. You'll see."

My future bedroom was the first at the top of the stairs, although it was probably too small to once have been the master bedroom. The furniture, as promised, was cheap and functional, with a small desk and chair, a heavily upholstered armchair with a few patches and slits on its leathery surface, a night table, and rows of empty bookshelves across the walls. Dropping my overnight bag on the bed, I sat down to test the springs. "It seems firm enough," I said, "and it doesn't make a lot of noise, either."

"A good thing," said Mark. "You don't want to keep us up all night if you get lucky."

He showed me the adjoining bathroom, which I would be sharing with him, and then the closet. "It's not big, but there's additional storage space in the small attic above Dan's room if you think you'll need it."

Dan's room was down the hall, where he had a private bath. Leonard slept on the first floor in what was once the dining room, and although he had his own sink and toilet, he had to come upstairs for a bath or shower.

"Of course, there's plenty of storage space in the basement, but we never go down there," Mark said as we descended the stairs. "I'll show it to you, though, if you want to see it."

I told him that I had to get back to the library, but that I did want to see the kitchen. I had always been fond of cooking, and one of the reasons I wanted to leave the dorm was so that I could again begin preparing food for myself. "And maybe for you guys, too, on occasion, if we can come to some kind of agreement."

It was a spacious kitchen, with a deep pantry, a large built-in cabinet on one side, and a broom closet in the corner. The refrigerator was also large, with a separate freezer below and the motor audibly running. The floor was covered with a worn green linoleum that might have been original with the house, and it was soft and uneven, as if the floorboards beneath it were warped and rotting.

Leonard had preceded us into the kitchen. He was standing by an old steel and porcelain gas range, and as he waited for the water in his teakettle to boil, he was turning the dials to the other burners on and off, as if he were testing them to see how high he could make the flames rise. Behind this heavy white stove, on the bare plaster wall—the shade of yellowed parchment—was a wide amorphous discoloration, like a puddle splashed across it, reminding me of the tenacious grease stains above the deep fryers in my favorite Chicago diners.

"This is great," I said. "I can't wait to get my hands dirty."

"Good. We'll be sure to leave you plenty of space in the fridge. Would you like to join us tonight for dinner?"

"Sure," I said, "and I can help out here in the kitchen if you like."

"It's Wednesday," said Leonard, who had stopped fiddling with the burners and had begun listening to us. "We stay out of the kitchen on Wednesday nights."

"That's right," said Mark. "We order takeout on Wednesdays."

"We stay out of the kitchen on Wednesday nights," repeated Leonard. "Wednesday night is extermination night."

"Extermination night?" I asked.

"More like extermination eve," Mark said, gripping my arm, and he began to lead me out of the kitchen. "But we'll explain that to you tonight. Pizza, okay? Sausage?"

"Sure, but…"

Mark stopped suddenly, his attention drawn to something on the floor. Bending over, he picked it up and brought it into the light. It was like a tiny transparent cartridge that had once held medicinal particles or powders.

"An egg capsule?" asked Leonard.

"Yeah."

"Empty?"

"Yeah."

"You've got roaches?" I asked.

"This is Chicago, isn't it?" replied Mark.

***

Dan had joined us for dinner in the living room, and he explained "extermination night" to me as Mark and Leonard ate their pizza slices, sipped their beers, licked their fingers, listened, and nodded in agreement.

"To put it bluntly," Dan said, "we've got sort of a roach problem, although perhaps the word 'problem' is overstating the case. I'm sure it's not a problem to them, for example."

Dan, like Mark, was training to be a geneticist, and although like all good biologists he did not anthropomorphize other species, he was not above seeing things from a lab animal's perspective. Of course, counting fruit flies all day would have been more than enough to turn me forever against all insect life. But Dan had grown up with the redwoods practically in his backyard, and every summer Mark returned to his family home in Montana to fish in the mountain streams, and nothing, it seemed, could subvert their inbred love for natural things.

Yet, although both could empathize with a fruit fly or a cockroach, neither was enthusiastic about sharing their living quarters with them.

"But an infestation shouldn't be your problem," I said. "It's the owner's responsibility. She needs to call in an exterminator."

"We don't want an exterminator," said Dan. "They use powerful, toxic chemicals, dangerous to the environment at any level. You have heard about the ravages of DDT, of course?" and he looked at me like an archbishop eyeing a newly converted acolyte just in from the pagan territories. He continued, "They use chemicals like chlorpyrifos and diazinon, and you don't want to be responsible for spreading that kind of stuff into the biosphere, do you? So, we take care of it ourselves on a regular basis, once a week."

"What, with cans of Raid?"

"That's no better. We weren't put on this earth to poison it."

"We do it by hand," said Mark.

"Tonight," said Leonard. "Or, rather, tomorrow morning."

"Listen," I said. "I may need to rethink this. I may not want to move into a house infested with roaches."

"This house is not infested with roaches," said Dan. "We've

done a damn good job of containing them. You won't see them anywhere, except maybe in the kitchen, and even there only infrequently."

"They like the kitchen," said Leonard.

"It's not really a question of liking," said Dan. "They're naturally inclined to nest there, because that's where the food is, and the warmth, and the quiet darkness for most of the night, and then there's our little experiment…"

"We hardly ever see them anywhere else," said Mark. "Maybe they're in the basement, too, but we don't go down into the basement."

"Nobody goes down into the basement," said Leonard.

"But I like to cook," I said. "I'll want to use the kitchen."

"Don't worry about that," said Mark. "You won't see them during the day, and almost never in the evening, or even a large part of the night."

"It's like a controlled experiment in natural selection," explained Dan. "The house has always been rented by members of the Graduate Biology Department, and we've been able to eliminate them room by room through very systematic prophylactic measures, until we got them pretty much confined to the kitchen. In addition, over the years, not only have we limited the population to a single controlled community, we've selected one that seems to restrict its activities to just a few hours, deep in the night."

"Between two and four a.m., to be precise," said Leonard.

"So," said Dan, "once a week, at two fifteen a.m., Thursday morning, we sneak quietly down into the dark kitchen… None of us have classes early Thursday. Do you?"

"No," I said.

"Then we turn on the lights suddenly and have at them. Of course, we'll never completely eliminate them, but by culling the population that way, we keep it down to reasonable levels. For the most part, they are now no more than an invisible presence here."

"And you don't spray them? No Raid?"

"Paper towels, and shoes for the ones underfoot. Wear flat soles, by the way. Those ridged running shoes can get sloppy."

"It's like hand-to-hand combat," said Leonard. "Like ancient warfare."

"Leonard here likes to stand by the range and steer them into the burners," said Mark. "He likes to see them flare up and pop."

"Greek fire," said Leonard. "The Assyrians used something like it, and the Byzantines saved their empire with it. The ultimate weapon in the ancient world. Fire's the only way. It cauterizes. Purifies."

"Are you okay with this, then?" Mark asked me.

"I'm not sure," I said.

"Well, it all goes down pretty quick, and then we go to sleep, and mop it all up in the morning, and that's our way of keeping the kitchen clean, too. And then both sides pretty much forget about it, and keep out of each other's way, until the next Thursday morning at two fifteen. So, I'll knock on your door at two?"

"Okay," I said, returning my last half-eaten slice of pizza back into the box, "since I've already brought my stuff over for the night. I'll give it a try."

"See you at two, then," said Mark.

***

I tried to sleep sitting up in the easy chair, but I was still awake when Mark knocked on the door. He handed me a roll of paper towels.

"Weapon of choice," he said, and then told me to keep quiet and hold on to the banister as he led me down the unlit stairs. In the thick night, the house itself seemed to envelop us in the stillness of its years, but we were wearing shoes, and the staircase was old, and it creaked as we descended. Dan and Leonard, both also armed with paper towels, met us in the living room, and as we proceeded toward the kitchen, I noticed that Leonard was barefoot. He would not be using his feet as bludgeons, I guessed, and as three of us halted at the kitchen's threshold, he disappeared into its darkness, tiptoeing across its soft floor to position himself by the stove. The flash from its burners would be our signal.

Dan, Mark, and I waited, paper towels in hand. From one of the apartments across the alleyway, a murky, yellowish beam of light filtered across our faces, outlining dim shadows against the walls. Mark slid his arm slowly inside the kitchen, groping for the light switch. "You wait here at the door," he whispered in my ear. "Make sure none of them get past you. Then work the walls."

Four gas flames fired up in quick succession at the far end of the kitchen. "Now," Mark cried out as he turned on the light. Dan rushed toward the center of the room, stomping hard on the floor with each step, and when he reached the table there, he began pounding its surface with paper towels. At the same instance, Mark headed to the buffet affixed to the cabinet, occasionally veering from his path to stamp a foot, and once there—holding a paper towel and frequently flinging it to the floor as he ripped another one from the roll—he began pumping his fist downward as if it were a piston.

It took a moment for my eyes to become accustomed to the sudden brightness, and at first I noticed nothing more unusual than a vague sense of motion on all the surfaces, but very quickly the motion seemed to concentrate into forms, materializing as if sudden bursts of imperceptible winds were blowing in every direction, sending waves of oblong black pellets skittering across the walls and the floor.

But these were not pellets or pebbles, and some were speeding towards me. I quickly raised a foot and stomped down on the first, and something hard and brittle popped beneath my shoe like an unripe pistachio nut. And then another rolled between my legs too quickly for me to react. From the corner of my eye, I caught sight of two black shapes coursing down the wall beside me, and not having time to grab a towel, I smashed both against the plaster with a bare fist, one right after the next. As I rubbed the side of my hand against the roll beneath my arm, removing whatever was clinging to it, I noticed another pair driving towards me. The first I kicked with the point of my shoe, sending it flying back into the kitchen, and the second almost got past me, but it was bigger and slower than the others, and its viscera and whatever was in the egg capsule at its tail spurted out like white paste beneath my shoe and between the fringes of the living room carpet next to me. I turned back around to see another one rush past.

Dan was now working the chairs, and Mark had left the buffet to punch the walls and stomp on the floor, and then he followed something into a corner, kicking the floorboard brutally, as if in frustration at having just missed his prey.

From the range, I could hear a dull ping each time Leonard stabbed one of its metallic side panels. Earlier the top of the stove looked as if bullets of coal were tumbling across it, and many of them Leonard steered into the burners where they flared briefly into tiny pillars of light. Suddenly dropping to his knees, Leonard cupped something into his hands, stood up, and tossed another into the flame. He swiveled around a bit, looking for more, and then finding nothing he shrugged his shoulders and turned off the burners slowly, one after the next.

As if this, too, were a signal, both Mark and Dan straightened up, Mark rubbing both sleeves of his shirt with his hands and then shaking his arms as if he feared something might have crawled inside.

"That's it," said Dan.

"You see, it doesn't take long," said Mark. "Not very big, are they, but they are fast."

"Yeah," I said, failing to admit that at least one and perhaps two or more of them had been quick enough to get past me and escape into the living room.

"And you only see them between two and four a.m.," said Dan. "Fast and time sensitive. An experiment in natural selection."

"Unnatural selection," said Mark, raising his depleted roll of towels in triumph.

Shreds of tissue paper were scattered across the kitchen, some oddly solid and motionless as if glued to the walls, the floor, the furnishings, as if shrouding the victims of the night's carnage. Elsewhere splotches of organic matter lay open, often that same white paste I had seen beneath my own shoe, here and there flecked with bits of black or brown chitin. Charred pellets, some still glimmering like fading embers, lay on and around the stove. Fragments of exoskeleton and vestigial wings were scattered about, and although it was probably just my imagination, I could have sworn I noticed an occasional antennae fluttering like a string in a breeze or a spiny leg attached to the fragment of a thorax, uplifted and quivering in a final agony. The insect equivalent of the aftermath of a great battle, I thought—Antietam, the Marne—littering the field with its dead.

"Turn off the light," said Dan. "We'll clean it all up in the morning. For now, let's get some sleep."

Mark switched off the light, but there must have still been some gas leaking from the burners, since a pale blue glow, slowly descending, hung over the oven, and the weak light filtering in from the apartment next door must have been strong enough to throw a dim shadow against the wall above the range.

"What's that!" I cried out.

"What?"

"There, there on the wall!"

"What?"

I struggled to find the light switch without success. "Turn on the fucking light!"

Mark switched the light back on. He turned his eyes to the wall where I was staring.

"There's something here," I said. "I saw something on that wall, like a huge shadow, only it was denser, and it was growing and shifting, like flames rising from a fire, only it seemed almost solid. It was shifting at its edges, like hundreds of filaments, like, what do you call it, cilia, or the tiny legs of centipedes." I looked around. "There's something in here with us."

"It's the stain on the wall," said Leonard. "That's what you were looking at."

"No! I saw it expanding and moving, as if it were reaching out, toward us."

"It's late," said Mark. "It's that grease stain. You were probably nodding off, dreaming of something or other."

"No," I said angrily and with all the conviction of a witness to an alien abduction. "There was something else in here, with us."

"Let's get some sleep," said Dan. He turned the light off.

But I didn't sleep that night, particularly after I thought I saw something out of the corner of my eye running swiftly across the sheet of my bed and towards my pillow and then beneath it. I sat up, instead, in the easy chair with the lights on, trying to read, although just after sunrise, I nodded off.

A few hours later, I packed whatever I had unpacked and left for good.

***

When I returned to my dorm room that morning, I unpacked again very carefully, although I had considered taking the bag and its contents outside and burning it all, and perhaps I should have, because that very same night, I continued to see, just out of the line of my vision, tiny black objects coursing across my blanket, my desk, my walls, scurrying beneath cushions, my blotter, under floorboards, and into dark corners. I'm sure they were all products of my imagination, easily exposed as such in the light of day, but from that night, I began having trouble sleeping, and once I did fall asleep, the dreams began.

Most were typical nightmares, like horror movies, the expected kind, with massive insects, larger than the largest tropical species, or teeming swarms emerging from toilets, drains, dark alleyways, and sometimes from unexpected places like from the pages of a cookbook or from a girlfriend's mouth prior to a kiss. As I moved from place to place over the years, I took my roaches with me, both the imaginary and the real ones, and I wondered at times if I had become the roach equivalent of Typhoid Mary. Eventually, after many years, the dreams went away, descending from their peaks, with monsters the size of Dobermans, their carapaces huge and heaving, to an occasional marauder or two easily dispatched with a spray from my can of Raid, and, yes, I had no compunction about equipping myself with an extensive arsenal of chemical weaponry, both in my dreams and in real life.

Years later, I wondered if I had become a host for a particle or an offspring of that presence, that material shadow I had felt lurking there in that kitchen with us, carrying a semblance of it down the years along with me. At the time, of course, I never would have considered such a thing, since I had assumed that, whatever it was, it had been destroyed by the horrible inferno that incinerated the house.

***

Mark called me the morning after the fire. He and Dan had been working late in the lab, and they had returned together that night to find the entire street cordoned off by the fire department, helpless before the wall of flames in front of them, but intent on protecting the neighboring structures. Another roommate for the empty room had not yet been found, and first it was thought that nobody had been harmed, until the next day when Leonard's corpse was discovered in the basement.

He may have been trapped there when the fire broke out, although what he would have been doing in the basement was a mystery, or his body may have simply fallen through when the floor above collapsed. What was clear, however—and this was a small consolation—he had died from smoke inhalation.

"I was really sorry about it," said Mark when we got together the day after Leonard had been found. "But I never really got to know the guy very well. He kept pretty much to himself, and, you know, we were always in the lab. I met his dad once. He was kind of weird, like him."

"You don't think Leonard had anything to do with…"

"No, of course not. The fire department is pretty sure it was some sort of seeping gas leak. Maybe he left one of the burners on. They think it started in the kitchen, and all that accumulated grease gave it a pretty good kick. It spread fast."

"I don't want to sound flippant," I said, "but at least the roach problem's been solved." My roach dreams had started that week, and they had been very much on my mind.

"I'm not so sure about that," said Mark. "There are stories about the riots in the sixties, in those inner-city neighborhoods, that when an old tenement would go up in flames, waves, battalions of roaches could be seen migrating across alleys and empty lots and into neighboring structures, particularly the wooden ones."

"Like rats leaving a sinking ship?"

"More like army ants before a jungle fire. Roaches are communal creatures, you know, and under duress, they swarm… By the way, I'm going over there tomorrow morning to take a few pictures. I had some lab equipment in the room and some money, too, so I'll probably make an insurance claim. Do you want to come along?"

"Sure," I said, hoping that perhaps the sight of the ruined building would help subdue those nocturnal phantoms that were just then beginning to haunt my nights.

***

The house had been quickly consumed by the fire, and almost the entire structure had collapsed into the basement, raising a huge cloud of smoke and flames that resembled, according to several neighbors, the detonation of an aerial bomb. Charred beams stood like ruined telephone poles in the depression, and the empty frame of the cupola that had once loomed over the house now laid on its side above the debris like the rusted bridge of a tramp steamer shipwrecked on a reef. The front lawn and surrounding pavements were littered with blackened planks and brick, shards of slate and shingles, twisted circuitry, and puddles of metal molten into odd shapes, all covered with splotches of mud, soot, and a fine white drapery of powder that may have come from exploded glass.

Mark began to circle the property, taking shot after shot, finally halting in front of the east wall, which was still partially upright. The fragment of a gutter, hanging down from a thin metal thread, was swaying slightly in the soft breeze.

He crossed into the empty lot that separated the ruins from the neighboring house, which now looked even whiter and more pristine, and as Mark knelt to get a full shot, a car pulled up and parked in front of it.

It was a new Volvo, and its trunk was packed so full of cartons and luggage it had to be tied down with a cord coiled around its latch. A young man and woman stepped out from either side of the car, and the woman then turned around to help a young girl, maybe six or seven years old, unbundle herself from the back seat. When she hopped out, I noticed she had the same straw-colored hair—sweeping down past her shoulders—as the woman, whom I assumed was her mother, and the same high-rounded cheeks, tinged with pink. As the two stood there, with their backs to the car, they were joined by the man, and together they examined the house in front of them, wide smiles on their faces, as if they expected Mark to turn around and snap their picture, too. The man then removed a ring of keys from his pocket, rattling them for a moment like some sort of bell, and the little girl began to run up the sidewalk toward the house.

"Hold it!" the man cried out, and she stopped to look back at him. "First things first," and he strode over to the FOR SALE sign, plucking it out from the edge of the lawn.

MIDNIGHT RUN

She had to run despite the lateness of the hour and the frost in the air. All night she had watched those thin, icy fingers creeping up the window panes, forming their silvery, lacy webs as the frames shivered slightly in the wind, and she almost resisted the compulsion to run. But the glacial cold would also keep others inside, and on such nights, especially this night, she needed to be alone, even though she was well aware that venturing into those empty streets could expose her to the threat that had been terrorizing the city for the past two years.

Yet this last concern meant little to her since she had lived with a constant sense of fatality from the moment Eric had died. He had always insisted that he had never intended to infect her, that it had been an accident, that he would never do such a thing, but now that he was gone—and she began to consider their time together more dispassionately—she no longer believed him.

They had fallen in love almost from the day she had arrived at the research station in western Kenya, and from the very beginning Eric had identified a certain affinity between them. How often, she asked herself, had he declared that they were one and the same, body and soul. He had even tried to convince her to share his passionate belief in the animistic religions they were supposed to be studying, but that was a line she refused to cross. "You'll see," Eric promised, as he lay dying in front of her. "We're one in the same, and who we are transcends everything we know. Even this small world of ours. You'll see." But all she saw was that what had led to his death would surely lead to hers, and for that, she would never forgive him.

Once she had returned home, her anger and passion regularly erupted into a furious rage she could not control, and especially at those times she needed to be alone. Often, when the pressure became unbearable, she was obliged to run, running deep into the night and into the early morning hours, returning with the rising of the sun, weary and depleted but, relatively, at peace with herself.

She had always loved running. "You run like a girl! You run like a girl!" her brothers used to yell after her when she was very young, and perhaps that was the incentive she needed to train long and hard enough to qualify for two state championships in the middle distances. A torn Achilles tendon prevented her from competing in college, but although she could never regain the speed she had as a teenager, once her leg healed, she continued to run whenever she could. In fact, she had even registered for a local marathon and had begun intense training for distance and endurance, when she won that coveted research grant to study religions in Africa. Running the marathon and her doctoral dissertation would then have to wait for her return. And now, with her return, both were very unlikely to happen.

***

Although she never enjoyed running in the cold, she had become accustomed to it, and her gear, piled on the window seat covering the radiator, lay awaiting her. As she began to slip into her several pairs of fleecy sweats, she realized that the additional layers would not only provide sufficient warmth, but in flattening the contours of her body and concealing her gender, they would provide an extra touch of safety. It had clearly become dangerous for a woman to venture outside alone into the city at night. After the third murder, the papers had begun to notice, and by now the count had reached ten. Most of the victims had been walking the streets for professional reasons, but there was also a middle-aged housewife on her way to an all-night pharmacy to pick up a needed prescription for her disabled husband. A student ornithologist, in search of a rare owl, had been found in the wooded bird sanctuary, and in the past two months, a pair of young career women had been added to the list, one a lawyer, the other an investment banker, both of whom could find the time to jog only at night or in the pre-dawn hours. The first had been found in a dry creek bed crossing through Northern Park at the other end of the city, and the second in a ravine bordering the reservoir.

The ski mask she slipped over her hair and face would contribute to her anonymous appearance, and this she covered with a woolen cap, and over the cap, pressing it tightly against her temples, the hood of her sweatshirt. Still, she felt she had little to fear, since she was unlikely to encounter anyone on her nocturnal runs, even in warmer weather. The route she preferred to follow wound through a stretch of parkland largely abandoned by the municipal authorities and commercial interests. She would enter through a gate, which never seemed to be locked, and immediately turn into a side trail, bordered with dense shrubbery and lined with maples and elms whose branches arched low overhead. The path would lead her through a pair of underpasses, bringing her to the edge of an artificial lake that had been used for recreational boating. A pair of wooden docks—from which paddleboats and canoes had once been launched—had partially collapsed into the stagnant waters, complementing the remnants of a small bankrupt amusement park at the other side of the lake, its booths and sheds decaying along a short midway. The green surrounding the lake had turned largely into a swampy bog, but the path she would be following rose to higher and drier ground and then sharply descended into a long tunnel beneath the observatory through which a tram connecting the park to the center of the city had once run. From the tunnel she would cross over to another treelined path—this one edged primarily with poplars—that would bring her back to the gate, where she would begin again, adding further laps around the park until she was exhausted and the turmoil howling inside her had largely been silenced.

This night, as soon as she stepped over her building's threshold, the difference between the dry heat of the foyer and the glacial chill of the fresh air sent an uncontrollable shudder throughout her body. But it also invigorated her, and the shivering was quickly followed by a steady animal energy that quickly took her from a tentative jog to a quicker pace, far too rapid for the start of a long workout. After only five minutes, she was inside the park, and she slowed considerably as she headed down her usual path where the shadows seemed to welcome her, although this night she was surprised by the brightness of the moonlight, filtering through the linked branches and dead foliage overhead. Settling into her pace, she was comforted by the sharp crunch of the dried leaves that accompanied her every step.

But upon entering the first underpass, which ran beneath a wide boulevard that cut through the park, the crackling beneath her footsteps seemed to have doubled, as if they were casting a shadow of sound. Was this simply the pounding of her running resonating against the walls of the enclosed space, or had someone followed her inside? *Followed?* she thought, questioning herself. *And how paranoid is that?* and although she never expected to encounter anyone on a wintry night such as this, she was occasionally accompanied by a scattering of others, running and walking in both directions, in all seasons.

As she exited from the shaft, the echoing sound behind her diminished, but it had not faded away. Someone was behind her and gaining on her fast. She thought for a moment about disrupting her workout to look back over her shoulder, if only to give the other person a sense of her awareness, but the woolen cap and the hood over it blocked her peripheral vision, and to look around she would have to come to a complete halt, something she was reluctant to do. Just prior to reaching the second underpass, she slackened her pace, as if inviting the other runner to pass her before they entered the darkness and narrowness of the tunnel. But he—and now she was sure he was a man—also slowed down, although he was now close enough for her to hear that he was breathing heavily, as if he had been struggling to overtake her. Once inside the cavernous space, which extended beneath a row of boathouses, she increased her speed, and he did, too, as if he had found a second wind. But he failed to close the short distance between them, and she emerged back into the moonlight that sent pillars of illumination through the archway of entangled branches above her.

Maybe I should slow down again, she thought, *let him pass me and be done with this silliness. He can't even know I'm a woman.* and then in the fraction of the second, between the concussion at the back of her head that coursed through her nervous system like a bone-shattering electric shock and her momentary loss of consciousness, she heard her brothers yelling after her, "You run like a girl! You run like a girl!"

***

She didn't recall tumbling to the earth, but she must have instinctively braced her fall with her shoulder, since the soreness there was the first sensation she felt upon awakening. Flat on her back, she tried to prop herself up on her elbows, but her vision blurred as if her head were spinning, and she probably would have fallen back anyway even if the crushing weight pressing down on both of her shoulders hadn't forced her to the ground. When the rear of her head rebounded against the surface, she again almost lost consciousness.

"Don't fall asleep," he said, as the pressure from one of his knees turned the soreness in her shoulder into a sharp pain. "I want you to be awake for everything, and tonight, I can take my time, since it doesn't look like we'll be disturbed." He pulled off her woolen cap, and as he leaned forward, his shifting weight almost suffocated her.

"And, of course, we can't have this, can we?" he said, gripping the hem of her ski mask in both hands. "It gives me such pleasure, you know, to see the fear in a face," and then he ripped the mask off her head.

Instantly, he leaned back. "What have we here?" he said. "The bearded lady in the circus? Something from a freak show?" And then he realized what he had stirring beneath him, regaining full consciousness, and that the twisted rope coiled in his pocket—intended eventually to garrote his victim—would be far from sufficient to protect him. For her part, she regretted, for his sake, that he could not see the look of fear that he said gave him so much pleasure in his own face.

***

After finishing her lap around the park, she ended her run with a sweet taste in her mouth and only one additional regret. The blood on her sweats did not bother her, since those stains would disappear completely after several wash and spin-dry cycles. But she was truly sorry that the sharpness of her claws had ruined another fine pair of leather gloves.

VIXEN

I 've always loved the wilderness, despite the fact that—or perhaps because of it—the most traumatic event of my life, up until now, took place there. It was in the North Cascades, just on the fringe of the national park, an area devoid of recognized trailheads and managed campsites, and all it took was a fearless and independent Scoutmaster, a handful of devoted Eagle Scout candidates, a moonless night, the need to relieve myself, a campfire burning down to its embers, perhaps a slip and a fall or a simple wrong turn and disorientation, and a day and a half later, the silence of the forest was broken by the yelping of dogs and the drone of helicopters overhead. It became one of the longest search and rescue missions undertaken by the Skagit County Sheriff's Office, and even though the cadavers of two young men were found—one of them upstream a treacherous canyon river, the other downstream—neither of them were mine, and after almost three weeks, the effort was abandoned, and I was given up for dead.

It wasn't until almost the first onset of snow that I was discovered by a pair of hunters—Ian and Floyd—beneath a rock overhang, sheltered by a weave of twigs and leaves. My shirt, I was told, was held together with pine needles, my shoes matted with grasses and moss, and gnawed roots, acorn shells, and the bones of small mammals covered the ground around me. I was, apparently, too busy sharpening a branch with my Swiss Army knife to even notice Ian and Floyd as they approached.

I later learned that in the months following, membership of the Boy Scouts surged, and a survival group named a brigade after me. And yet I remember none of it. Absolutely nothing. Despite the entreaties of reporters and interviewers, I could not recall a single emotion I might have felt—hopes or fears—or even more material matters, how I found sustenance or sheltered myself. Not even the shred of a memory sufficient to fabricate the slightest of narratives. It was as if, rather than having fought daily to stay alive in the depths of a forest, I had been lying in a coma for weeks in a hospital bed, and then as soon as I awoke, whatever dreams and visions I may have had, no matter how vivid or deep, had vanished instantly like water through a sieve.

About all that I retained from my experience was, oddly enough, an even more intense attraction to the wilderness. The scent of pine and other natural life in the air, the crackle of dead foliage under-foot, the taste of berries and roots and other foods gathered raw, the flash of movement nearby, the songs of birds at dawn and the dead silence of midday, the streaks of pure color in the sunlight as if from the broad strokes of a painter's brush, the solitude, the uncertainty, the primal anticipation of danger all seemed to hold me with an even tighter grip. As soon as my divorce was complete, I closed on the Bradley Estate, a property at the edge of a deep forest on the downward slope just east of Boulder Springs, Washington.

Of course, that would have been the last straw for Dorothy, if the last straw had not already been laid down months before. I had been accused by my wife of "mental torment," although I assumed that was merely lawyer hyperbole for "incompatibility." In fact, the split had been rather amicable, with Dorothy getting most of our material possessions and with our financial holdings divided pretty much in half. I insisted on sole ownership of Wendy, but Dorothy had never been fond of cats anyway, and if, in fact, our marriage had lasted up to the move to Boulder Springs, my adoption of Vixen would have surely been another one of those final straws.

The Bradley Estate had been on the market for some time. The area around it had long been thought to be prime for development, but the recession earlier in the century ended all hopes for that, leav-ing behind several feeder roads heading nowhere and isolated lines of utility poles. Economic activity had generally been confined to the other side of Boulder Springs, with its vacation homes and re-sorts for skiers and hikers extending to the foothills of the North Cascades, although, fortunately, the Bradley Estate was close enough to town to have hooked up long ago with its electrical and water systems.

Actually, the Estate was hardly an "estate," but rather a single dwelling surrounded by several acres of cleared ground that had once been a private garden. The building was basically one story with a narrow, peaked attic space extending most of its length. It stood on a foundation of granite blocks cut from a quarry nearby, but the rest of the structure was wood with a verandah sweeping around most of the exterior. Wide and long and flat, it reminded me, from a distance, of a huge river barge, and at its prow, it opened into a spacious reception area that funneled into a corridor with partitioned rooms leading up to the kitchen. At the entrance to the kitchen, where the veranda ended on both sides, two turret-like projections bulged outward, both with floor-to-ceiling bay windows. One became my dining area, and the other, overlooking the forest, became my office.

Attached to the stern, as it were, of the barge was what the realtor called a "bonus," a large carriage house that once had had access from the main building but was now sealed up by the kitchen wall. Its windows were boarded, and the outer door, too, was sealed, although the realtor assured me that all I would need was a locksmith and a carpenter to convert it into a guest house, a garage, or an additional storage area. Later I was informed by the clerk at the grocery store that it once may have served as the final dwelling—or rather prison—of one of the Bradley children, a severely disabled autistic child with violent tendencies who had, apparently, lived and died there without ever having left the property. After his death, which was, according to the clerk, never reported, the family sealed the carriage house tight, and it has remained so ever since. "Of course, those are just rumors," the clerk said in reference to the Bradley kin. "And you know what rumors are, don't you? Just that. So many rumors."

The house was far too close to the forest for me to afford the insurance premiums but, in fact, I did not intend to stay there for long. I was there to write, to finish the third volume of my McElroy Murders trilogy. I had already gone through most of my advance, and it was imperative that I submit a final manuscript before, as my publisher warned me, everyone had forgotten who both I and the McElroys were. I had no doubt that, given my isolation and lack of distractions, I could finish the book by the end of the year, and once pre-pub sales were in, I could determine whether I wanted to hold on to the estate—to write my next trilogy, say—or return to the city once and for all.

Of course, I could not spend all day, every day writing, and most of my mornings were devoted to hour-long hikes through the depths of the forest. It was at the end of one of those walks that I found Vixen, or, rather, she found me.

The forest here was thick, dark, and ancient; it was also expansive, and once it had climbed the other side of the slope across the river, it swept around Boulder Springs to join the wilderness at the foot of the mountain range extending west. Since there were no trails to speak of, I marked my progress on the barks of trees with the blade of my Swiss Army knife, which I always kept razor sharp; I was not about to get lost again, especially since, other than my cat Wendy, there was nobody around to notice my absence. I usually carried a camera with me, since now that the construction crews were long gone, wildlife had returned in large numbers. Along with flocks of birds, both migratory and resident—owls, woodpeckers, falcons, and eagles—there were several varieties of deer, and even an occasional elk. As far as predators were concerned, I never saw anything larger than a black bear, although there were wolves, bobcats, coyotes, and others that fed off the growing populations of chipmunks and squirrels. Fortunately, at least according to the clerk at the grocery store, there had been no sightings of Bigfoot for several decades, although he did mention that a pair of wolverines had been spotted wandering around the lower slopes. "People on the east side of town," he told me, "generally do not let their pets run free," and although Wendy had access to an inner courtyard when we lived in the city, I decided then to keep her confined to the house.

I thought of those wolverines when, upon returning from one of my first hikes, I saw my front door shaking violently as if somebody, or something, were desperately trying to get inside. Approaching from beneath the veranda, I could not see what it was, so I climbed quietly up to one of the side entrances. When I turned the corner, I found a large feline scratching ferociously at the front door. Almost at once it noticed my shadow, but rather than flee into the woods as I had expected, it settled back on its haunches for a moment, as if in reflection, and then arose and approached, slowly and with caution. Once it reached me, it twirled its body around my ankles, purring loudly enough for me to hear while I stood upright. Falling to my knees, I quickly learned that she was a female as I probed her softly with my fingers. I failed to find any tag or collar, but when she wedged herself between my thighs and began to purr even more loudly, I assumed that she had been someone's house pet, now lost or abandoned.

She was larger than the typical short-haired mongrel, heavily striped with those jagged lines zigzagging across her face like tribal tattoos, and her yellowish brown coloring probably camouflaged her well in the forest, for although she seemed to be hungry, she was certainly not starving. In fact, she was a good deal heavier than Wendy—who was basically the same species although she had a little Persian in her and a much thicker coat—and I wondered if there was a bit of a bobcat in this one.

"All right," I said, as she continued to snuggle deeper into my thighs, "we'll give it a try, but it's Wendy's call, not mine." When I got up, she followed me to the front door, and as soon as I saw the depth of the ragged furrows she had scratched into its wooden panels, I realized what her name would be, a combination of the feral and the seductive. "You're quite the terrorist aren't you, you... you little vixen?" She meowed and accompanied me into the house.

Wendy usually came to greet me when I returned from my hikes, but perhaps having been frightened by the scratching at the door, she now was waiting for me across the reception area, and as soon as she saw Vixen, her hair climbed up her spine, and she hissed. Vixen, almost as if she realized what was at stake, lowered her body and, slowing her pace to a crawl, began to slink toward the other cat. When she reached the middle of the room, she stopped, her stomach almost down to the floor. Wendy approached, they touched noses, and after she circled Vixen twice, Wendy raised her tail high and headed for the kitchen. The other cat, as if eager to be given a tour of the premises, followed, and shortly thereafter I joined them to open a can of cat food and to grill a hamburger for myself.

From then on, the two seemed to get along, although at a distance. They never groomed one another, and Wendy chose to eat as far away from Vixen as possible. Wendy had her own scratch pole, too, and although I purchased an extra one for her new companion, Vixen preferred to concentrate on turning most of my second-hand furniture into sawdust. But from the time I bought a twin cat basket for Vixen and placed it near Wendy's in the warmest part of the reception area, they would often sleep together, although at night Wendy would sometimes settle into the cushions of the couch by my bed while Vixen prowled through the darkest corners of the house and into the narrowest of its hidden spaces.

I would also sometimes find the two of them sitting together, side by side, on the small bookcase in the reception area, staring out of the large picture window overlooking the forest, and on a few occasions, I was aroused from my desk by a howling cat scurrying and sliding across the floor. That would be Wendy, and when I got up to investigate, I would find Vixen still on the bookshelf, her tail swinging furiously back and forth, practically standing on her outstretched claws, scratching at the glass. She had probably seen a rabbit or some other small mammal crossing the lawn, but once—not very long ago—I was drawn from my desk by a vase crashing to the floor, and this time Wendy had run all the way into the kitchen to hide. The sun had already gone down, leaving the reception area dark, and when I turned on a desk lamp and pointed it toward the picture window, I found a pair of bright scarlet orbs of light flickering back at me. I had often been struck by the blank brightness of a cat's eyes suspended in midair like luminous disembodied buttons when struck by direct light, but they had always glimmered silver or white, never red, and I certainly intended to ask the vet about this oddity when I finally arranged to take Vixen into town for her rabies shots and to have her claws clipped down to the nibs.

That same night, I forgot to return the half pound of hamburger that I had been defrosting on the kitchen countertop to the refrigerator before going to bed. In the past, such neglect had never bothered me, since I would be cooking the meat the next day, and Wendy never seemed interested in sampling the kind of food I was eating. But that next morning, when I awoke, only a few shreds of beef and fat, intertwined with fragments of plastic wrap, remained of my meal. Vixen was sitting at the far end of the countertop, contentedly licking her paws, as if in triumph.

Before she could react, I grabbed her, tossed her into a closet, and after slipping in a bowl of water and a small open carton of kitty litter, I again slammed the door shut. "It's solitary confinement for you today, my lady," I said in a voice loud enough for her to hear, and walked back into the kitchen to see if I could find anything else to eat.

Yes, I know. It's sheer folly to think I could teach a cat anything by punishing it at random, but not only was I very angry, I was also ravenously hungry. I had neglected to go shopping that week, and it was Sunday, and all I had in stock were a couple of hamburger buns, a box of crackers, a half can of coffee, and a moldy head of lettuce. A six pack of beer provided me with some additional sustenance but, in general, both Vixen and I went to sleep later that night on empty stomachs.

When I awoke the next morning, Wendy was whining outside the closet door, and I had to lure her away with a tin of cat food. When she had finished, I cleaned out the bowl, filled it with the dry pellets that Vixen had always refused to eat, and placed it just outside the closet. "I'll let you out of solitary now, my dear," I said aloud, "but you're on bread and water for the day." And then I added, repeating what my vet in the city had once told me, "Besides, dry food's good for your teeth." When I opened the closet door, I expected Vixen to come plunging out in an almost invisible streak, but there was no movement from the inside, and as I bent over into the shadowy darkness, the sun rising behind my shoulders, to retrieve her water bowl, I saw only two specks of glittering red light, at eye level, staring back at me.

I have no idea when she finally left the closet, since I spent a good part of the day in town replenishing my provisions, and afterwards, I took a long walk in the forest, finally returning just before dark. I fed Wendy, but when I noticed that the bowl outside of the closet was still full of dry food, I said aloud, "I can be stubborn, too. That's all you're getting today!" I even expected Vixen to appear in the kitchen when I was grilling my hamburger. But I ate alone, and after a few hours of work on my manuscript, I went to bed.

I slept fitfully that night, awakened frequently by troublesome dreams, which I immediately forgot. But just after dawn I crept from beneath my sheets to find the house eerily silent. The cats rarely tried to wake me unless I had been sleeping exceptionally late, but no matter how early I decided to get out of bed, I could usually sense stirring somewhere within the house. As I emerged into the corridor outside my bedroom, the silence seemed to deepen, although when I reached the reception area, I found Vixen sitting on the bookcase, quietly licking her paws. Wendy, her back to me, was still peacefully asleep in her basket.

"Okay, breakfast, you two," but when I kneeled to awaken Wendy, I noticed that the blanket beneath her was drenched in blood. Drawing closer, I saw that her viscera, mangled and gnawed, had spilled from an abdomen that had been sliced cleanly open from the sternum to her pelvis.

By the time I stood up, stepped back a few steps, and turned around, Vixen had disappeared.

It took me most of the day to bury Wendy. The grave had to be deep enough to protect her from the scavengers in the nearby forest, but it also had to be wide enough to contain her basket, which acted as sort of a coffin. Wendy had been fond of her bed, but I wasn't burying her in it for sentimental reasons; rather, it was simply easiest for me to leave her where she was and wrap her and the basket up tightly together in one of the linen tablecloths Dorothy had left behind. And then I deposited my cat into her final resting place.

When I returned from the burial, the house seemed empty, and even though I opened a can of her favorite flavor, Mariners Catch, Vixen never reemerged from the shadows that day.

By the next morning the bowl had been licked clean, and even though I refilled it almost immediately, Vixen remained secluded wherever she had been hiding. Finally, late in the afternoon, when I rose from my desk to make a pot of coffee, I found her sitting at the threshold of my office. She was staring up at me, but before I could make a move towards her, she fled down the hallway.

My writing had not been going well, and after brewing my coffee, I settled down in the reception area with an Elmore Leonard book in hand to see if I could ease my mind. Vixen, always keeping her distance, was now intent on roaming along the perimeter of the space, as if she were searching for something, and I lifted my eyes often from my reading to watch her continue her hunt down the corridor and then through the partitioned rooms and finally into the kitchen. She repeated that same circuit over and over again, always, it seemed, with one eye on me, and if I stood up to refill my cup of coffee or even to stretch my body, she retreated quickly, as if she knew what she had done and feared retribution.

After returning to my desk in the evening, I soon found myself surrounded once again, by bunches of crumpled paper, and when I finally retired to the bedroom, I fell asleep sitting up on the couch, exhausted from my failed attempts to rekindle my imagination or to recapture the train of thought that had been disrupted by the events of the previous days.

When I woke an hour or two later, I found Vixen settled deep between my thighs, purring gently. I stroked her a few times, told her, "We needed to talk in the morning," and then got up to change. Once I had slipped between the sheets, she joined me in the bed, something she had never done before, as if she were now reluctant to leave me, although when I turned off my reading lamp and shifted to my side, I heard her drop to the floor and scamper from the room.

I again slept only until the early morning hours, and when I awoke it was to that same eerie silence that had disturbed me two days before. But that was understandable since I now had only one cat, and with her constant searching and wandering of the previous day, she was probably just as exhausted as I had been. So, I wasn't surprised to find Vixen still asleep in her basket, curled up with her back towards me. As I approached her, I made some clattering noises with the can against the porcelain bowl in my hand so that I wouldn't frighten her out of what appeared to be a deep sleep. But she didn't move. I bent down, and after I touched her shoulder, her body tilted slightly over, and when her head fell across the side of the basket, I saw that her eyes were wide open and that her tongue was dangling between her teeth out of the side of her mouth. As with Wendy, her intestines, also ravaged, were splayed across her sleeping basket in a pool of blood.

Before closing on the Bradley Estate, I had insisted that the realtor, at the seller's expense, hire the best extermination firm in the state to ensure that no vermin had since infested the property, and perhaps even more important, considering its proximity to the forest, that it was secure from all intruders. The last thing that I needed while trying to complete my manuscript was a family of raccoons or squirrels nesting and scurrying above me in the attic.

As soon as I had finished burying Vixen—in a grave right next to Wendy—I called that same pest control firm, and it took almost every last penny I had in the bank to persuade them to come up from the city the following day for a complete inspection of the house. It was almost the same team from a few months before, and it didn't take them very long to inform me that nothing much had changed from their previous visit. There was a new, small termite infestation beneath one of the veranda doors, and a few moths were found fluttering around in the attic—which they then fumigated—but other than myself, there was, they assured me, no other living presence inside the house. All access points were still secure, and nothing much larger than a mosquito could invade unless I neglected to close a door or a window. Before they left, however, I asked them to inspect the carriage house, but they insisted that any entrance through—or even under—the kitchen wall was impossible, and that since every opening on the outside of the carriage house—windows and doors, all of which had metal frames—had been soldered shut, they would need to demolish a portion of its structure to gain entry, and that they refused to do.

Once they were gone, I grabbed the pickax from the storage room and brought it into the kitchen. When I reached the wall that separated it from the carriage house, I swung the pickax over my head. But after a moment's hesitation, I let it drop to the floor. I had decided to put the Bradley Estate back on the market as soon as I submitted my manuscript, and although I could probably count on loans from friends and further advances from my publisher to support me before the book was published, I certainly could not finance the reconstruction of a structural wall. I would leave it up to others to explore whatever mysteries lay within the confines of a carriage house under seal.

Before going to sleep that night, I left a half pound of hamburger on the countertop to defrost. In the morning it was gone, the plastic wrap surrounding it torn into shreds.

The following day, I went into town to restock my freezer and pantry. The grocery clerk noticed that I had not purchased any cat food.

"They're gone," I said. "Both of them. Dead."

"Wolverines?" he asked.

"No. Something else. I buried them toward the edge of the forest. I think they'll be happy there."

"I'm sure they will," said the clerk. "Provided the Indian spirits don't mind."

"The Indian spirits?" I asked

"What, didn't the realtor tell you?" he replied. "That's sacred ground out there, or at least some people think it is. Chinook, where some of their most heroic and savage warriors were said to be buried long ago. On certain nights, drums have been heard beating just beyond the forest wall. Haven't you heard them?"

"Drums?" I asked.

"Or maybe they're just woodland noises. You never know about these things, do you? Drums. Bigfoot. Noises. Rumors. Just so many rumors... By the way, not to seem too nosey, but you sure like your hamburger, don't you?"

I smiled weakly and nodded, having no desire to tell him that I had lost much of my appetite and that most of the hamburger was not for me.

I began leaving a half pound out every other night, and by morning, it was always gone.

One night I stayed awake, sitting in one of the kitchen's shadowy corners, with a gun in hand, but whatever was eating my hamburger seemed to sense my presence, and the meat remained on the countertop untouched until I slipped it back into the refrigerator and I finally went to bed. On another night, I fell into a deep sleep on the stool right there next to the pantry; when I awoke several hours later, oddly enough, I was lying prone on top of my blanket and, of course, upon my return to the kitchen, except for some remnants left behind, the countertop was empty.

I suppose that most reasonable people under such uncertain circumstances would have long since departed for somewhere else. But I'd pretty much run out of money, and where could I go? Besides, I was still comfortable writing in my office there, and my work was again producing good results. During the day, even as winter approached, I had lengthened my walks in the forest, but since I continued to have difficulty sleeping, I often wrote deep into the early morning hours. In fact, as long as I left my offering on the kitchen countertop every other night, I did not feel especially threatened… until about a month ago.

That morning, when I awoke, I found the walls and floor of the kitchen splattered with fragments of the meat I had left out, as if the package had exploded or, rather, been shredded before being devoured in a fit of violent rage. Two nights later, I increased the portion by a quarter pound, and in the morning, everything had returned to normal, with only a few grease spots left behind.

I'm now working on my last two chapters, but I haven't really revised very much, and I fear that the entire manuscript will require significant and lengthy editing before I can submit it. Ordinarily, this would be normal practice for me and not much of a concern, but just the other morning, I again woke to find a portion of my offering sprayed across the kitchen with even more fury than before, the floor slippery with fat, the ceiling dripping with meat. The next night I left a full pound out, and in the morning I needed to do no more than wipe the countertop clean with a few swipes of my sponge.

Since then, I've transferred my 9mm Glock pistol from the

drawer of my night table to beneath my pillow when I go to sleep, and I have also begun to cuddle up in bed with a loaded shotgun by my side, which, by the way, I've named Dorothy. I realize that, even with such an armament, I would have little chance against something that could pounce upon two sleeping cats and eviscerate them without them hardly stirring. But still, I find the Glock and Dorothy to be comforting, and they help me to sleep, although I am becoming increasingly concerned that whatever it is that I am feeding in my kitchen every other night seems to be getting bigger and growing hungrier.

THE THEATER OF INFINITE DELIGHT

Only one couple is in front of us by the time we reach the ticket booth of the newly opened Red River Canyon Mystery Tour, quite a contrast from the anxious crowd that had been blocking our way just beyond the head of the Escarpment Trail on the other side of the park. So, despite the lateness of the afternoon and our growing impatience, we decided to climb the steps and purchase tickets for the Tour.

***

Twenty years before, shortly after we were married, my wife Diane and I were the only ones to hike along that narrow Escarpment Trail winding across the stony face of the mountainous bluff overlooking the gorge below. Through the arches and channels grooved into the granite and sandstone over many millennia by wind and the river now out of sight on the canyon floor, the trail eventually led us to a wide grassy plateau, which soon sloped down to the rippling waters of one of the Red River's many tributaries. Its banks were lined with birches and willows, and under one of those willows, between sips of Bordeaux, we spent the rest of the afternoon nibbling on bread and assorted cheeses as beams from the lowering sun filtered through the pendulous leaves to shimmer against the surface of the stream flowing beneath us.

But this time, we had brought neither bread nor wine, and although we knew there had been considerable development in the area since our last visit, we had hoped to hike the path in some degree of isolation, if only to recover a hint of that beauty and tranquility we had experienced two decades before.

But it was not to be. From the moment we were on the trailhead, we were accompanied by a pair of couples and a family of four, and just before we reached the first panoramic overhang, our progress was blocked by a wall of shifting bodies.

"Bikers ahead!" someone upfront explained.

"What's that?" commented a woman next to me who did not consider that to be an explanation.

"They're partying at the first overlook," came the reply, "and hardly anyone's getting through."

I recalled the perilous footing of the path crossing the scenic overview and also that a convention of motorcycle clubs was convening that weekend in a small town just over the state line, and we all watched as a volley of beer cans were launched overhead, arching into the air where, as the sun gleamed off of them, they seemed to hang suspended for a moment, before plunging into the chasm below.

"I hope those cans are empty," commented the women next to me. "Someone down there could get hurt."

"Don't worry, no one's allowed on the canyon floor," I said, recalling that hiking by the river was strictly prohibited due, as we had once been informed by a park warden, to the multiple threats of mud slides, flash floods, venomous snakes, and a variety of other natural dangers.

"Not anymore," said her companion. "It's open now and just teeming with folks."

"Let's get out of here," said Diane, pulling me away from the crowd. "Something should be done about all these superfluous people." A callous remark from a woman who was usually a caring person, but it was not unexpected. Diane had been a long-time member of the Sierra Club and had recently joined SGW! (Stop Global Warning!). She was not unsympathetic to the plights of others, but she was also concerned about massive overconsumption and uncontrolled population growth, and, in fact, she had recently called off a proposed Italian vacation for fear of being overwhelmed by the tourists in Florence, the Vatican, and Piazza San Marco.

"I'm sorry," she said in apology for her crassness, "but I was suffocating back there," and she hurried me along as if in escape from the presence of others as we descended toward the parking lot. But then I stopped her at that gate that had once prevented all entry down to the valley floor.

"Look," I said. It had swung open.

"What?"

"Don't you remember? There were chains last time we were here. Locked up tight. And there was a sign, something like, 'Hazardous Passage. Access Forbidden.'"

The sign linked to the iron piping now advised only, *Proceed at Your Own Risk.*

A couple crossed in front of us and through the gate. Both were about half our age, blonde and smiling, their cheeks pink and pudgy. I noticed he was slightly obese, his shirt hanging loose and flapping over his chino shorts. He was wearing sandals, and her feet were bare. I recall that the park warden from before had also warned us about the thorny brambles often closing in on the various trails, the shifting and unstable rocks beside the river and streams, the stinging insects.

"You sure you want to go down there?" I called out after them as the gate swung back. "They say it can be treacherous."

"Don't worry about us," he said over his shoulder. "We've got a GPS and plenty of water," and he raised a plastic bottle from a pouch looped across his stomach.

"We're seasoned hikers," she added as they began their descent. To them, I'm sure, the swinging gate was the opening to an adventurous experience, but to me it seemed more like a jaw clamping shut.

"Good luck," I said, almost beneath my breath as Diane pulled me along as if she feared I was tempted to join them.

"Do you still want to go to that funhouse?" she asked as we arrived at the parking lot, and she gestured over toward the mesa that seemed to sprout directly from the prairie on the opposite side.

"Why not? We've come this far, and if it's not too crowded, we should at least give it a look."

"Okay," and shrugging her shoulders, she followed as we worked our way through the sea of cars.

From a distance, the structure could barely be distinguished among the rocky outcroppings on the steep ridge of the mesa facing us. But as we approached, the details became more distinct. A pair of wide Doric columns was topped by a pediment extending between them, all carved into the stone in high relief to give the appearance of an archaic portico, the entrance to a temple or tomb recently unearthed from some ancient civilization. Behind it, in the shadow of the excavation, a dual series of columns, also etched from the wall, seemed to lead deep into the mountain.

The Red River Canyon Mystery Tour was chiseled in block letters into the shelf just above the pediment, and within that empty space itself—something that no ancient could ever have imagined—was the inscription, streaming in intermittent, multicolored, fluorescent bursts, *Enthralling! Entrancing! Captivating!*

The ticket booth was freestanding, like a miniature baptistry, set just inside the portico as if as an afterthought. It was clearly fabricated out of concrete plastered over with a stucco to simulate red sandstone, and I wondered, for a moment, if the entire mesa were an artificial construct, although it seemed natural enough even at close quarters. "Let's buy a ticket," I said. "There's only one couple ahead of us, and if it's crowded inside or if it doesn't look interesting, we can always leave." Diane reluctantly agreed and we climbed the graven steps together.

***

As we walk past the rows of columns, also incised out of the rock, I have the impression that we are entering a massive cavern, and I expect to see stalagmites and crystal formations projecting outward when we pass through the doors. But once inside, I feel, rather, that we are in a huge mine shaft, one illuminated by dim beams of light projecting from floor and ceiling, forming thick shadows everywhere that make it difficult to determine the height and depth of the space.

To the right, their faces barely discernible in the dimness, men, women, and children wait in a line that seems to plunge endlessly into the depths of this central gallery. A small swinging gate and an attendant wearing overalls and a miner's helmet blocks their entry into the tunnel behind him. An arrow painted next to him with the message *Plan of Visit* points inside, and curving over the tunnel are the words *Theater of Infinite Delight.*

Two lights flicker from the inside, and the man lowers the arm he had been extending to hold back the group at the head of the line.

"Okay, you're next," he says, taking their tickets, and after allowing them to pass through, he proceeds a step or two behind the group into the tunnel, switches the headlamp on his helmet on and off, and then returns back to the front of the line. "Next tour of five, or six if you're together. Children must be accompanied by adults," and as he silently counts heads to confirm the number, I approach.

"Excuse me," I ask, "how long—"

"Not long," he replies, cutting me off with the courteous impatience of someone who has been asked the same question too many times during the day. "We're speeding things up. We'll be closing before too long." And after telling the next group to, "Have your tickets ready, please," he looks back toward the tunnel to await the next flicker of lights.

I rejoin Diane. "He said—"

"I heard him. No."

"Come on, Diane. Only a couple of minutes to see how it goes. In the meantime, we can look around for a bit…" and then I nod toward a corridor just to the other side of the main entrance that probably serves for the coat check and the restrooms. "Over there, down that hallway, for instance, there's probably even a café…."

"And what's that?" she asks, indicating another tunnel directly across from us, with a similar gate at its front but without signage or an attendant. "I'll bet that's the exit," she continues, "where the tour ends. Let's take a look inside to see if it'll be worth a wait."

I nod and smile, recognizing that the suggestion comes from a woman who cannot pick up a mystery or detective novel without reading the final chapter first.

The gate swings open, unlocked. Once we are inside, the passage shifts very slightly to the left, and before long our view of the opening behind is obscured. As we move forward the shadows become even thicker, making it progressively more difficult to take in much around us. But, on the other hand, there doesn't seem to be anything worth seeing among the dark display cases, one right after the other in an almost numberless sequence, and, as we progress further along, the empty platforms where spectacles or shows of some kind could be staged.

"Maybe it all lights up and things happen when a tour passes through?" Diane suggests, but before I can reply, I stumble over an obstacle of some sort and, failing to keep my balance in the open space, fall to my hands and knees.

"What was that?" I ask.

"Rails," she says as she approaches to help me up.

"I guess a ride of some sort?" I wipe my hands on my jacket as I get to my feet.

"Look, it's only going to get darker, and we're probably in the middle of something under construction. Besides, we don't belong here, so let's go back and go home."

"I'm beginning to think you're right," but then I almost lose my balance again as the ground seems to shift beneath us.

"What's that?" I wonder aloud, and the thought of being trapped inside something like a collapsing mineshaft during an earthquake enters our minds simultaneously.

"Yeah, let's get out of here." But before we can take another step, the ground again groans and wavers, and just as we are thrown against the stony surface at our backs, we stare in amazement as across from us, amid an additional creaking and rumbling, a narrow sliver of illumination appears from ceiling to floor, widening to become a stream of blinding light as a portion of the opposite wall swings open like a revolving door. As it continues onward, to crash backward against the opposite wall, a man and a small girl stagger out from the depths of the brightness, and when the panel swings back hard on rebound, the pair of them stumble hastily forward into the passageway to avoid being struck by it. It slams shut, and we are again left in semidarkness.

"Could this be part of the tour?" Diane, drawing nearer to me, asks.

The man apparently hears her, and turning abruptly, his eyes blinking as if trying to adjust to the change in light, he crosses over to me to clutch at my jacket. The girl, as if afraid to be left by herself, follows and clings just as tightly to his trousers,

"I don't think so," I say in reply to my wife as I stare directly into the man's desperate eyes, and before I can demand an explanation from him, he blurts out, "How long have you been here? Inside, I mean?"

I push him softly away to keep his sour breath at arm's length. His cheeks are dark, as if he is intending to grow a beard, and his hair is as disheveled as his shirt and trousers. I am tempted to ask him, among other things, why he wants to know, but that same wild look in his eyes impels me to give him a straight answer.

"We just got here," I say. "Practically, anyway. We wanted to join a tour group, but then… In any case, we're thinking about…"

He draws uncomfortably close to me again. "You'll take us there? You'll show us where you came in!"

This sounds to me more like a command than a request, and I am reluctant to give him the satisfaction of immediate compliance. "Well, I don't know about that. Like I said, my wife and I just got here. We bought tickets, and frankly they weren't cheap…"

"I'll make it worth your while," and after withdrawing his wallet from his pocket, he stuffs a twenty-dollar bill into my hand.

"Look, that's not really necessary," and I offer him his money back. "Actually, we were heading back in that direction anyway. We don't need—"

"Keep it. Just show us where you came in." The little girl begins to tug more forcefully at the man's trousers. "Daddy, I've got to pee again."

"And hurry," he says, but before I can reply, he places his hand on my shoulder, and in a far gentler voice, he adds, "Please."

I nod, and after I take Diane's arm, we begin to retrace our steps, the father and daughter a short distance behind. Although the darkness does not seem to diminish as we proceed forward, perhaps my eyes have become more accustomed to the lack of light as I notice for the first time several deep crevices in the wall, almost the size of additional passageways themselves. The empty display cases seem more distinct, but there also seem to be less of them than there were before, and eventually they disappear completely.

"Shouldn't we be there by now?" Diane asks after a few more long minutes, and the man, apparently having overheard her, catches up with us. "What's that you said?" he asks.

I don't say anything as we stop, confronted by what appears to be a slight fork in the passage. A narrow shaft to the left seems to descend slightly into an even deeper pool of darkness, and to our right, a diffuse illumination beckons to us from some distance away. Naturally, without a word, I choose the path to the right, and I certainly breathe more easily when it leads us to the gate.

Hurrying forward, I push through it to step into the wide, central gallery. "And here we are," I say decisively.

"I don't know," says Diane as she joins me. "Something doesn't seem quite right."

"Of course not, it's empty," I reply, having realized that the line extending from the entrance to the theater across from us, along with the attendant, have vanished. "I guess he wasn't kidding about moving things along. It looks like they've all begun the tour, just like he promised. I wonder if there's still time for another one."

But the father, now also at my side, clearly has no interest in joining a tour, and he is again pulling at my jacket. "The entrance? Where you came in?"

"Right over there," I say, and with a sudden burst of energy, he launches himself towards the series of doors a few yards to my right, crashing against the first one. It does not budge.

"You've got to pull, not push," I call out, recalling that they opened to the inside. "I'm sure of that."

But when he tugs violently at the handle, the door still does not move. Trying the other three in turn, he pulls hard at each handle, and then, at the final one, he again bangs his shoulder several times against the door until the wall itself trembles. Finally, still clutching the handle, with his weight leaning against the door, he slides gradually downward to his knees.

His daughter, who has remained behind with us, gazing at his futile efforts in horror, runs up to him, and grabbing at his shirt, she cries out, "Daddy, I've got to pee! Now!"

Diane follows her, and with the stricken look on her face of someone who desperately wants to help but doesn't quite know how, she lays her hand gently on the girl's head. "Listen, honey, when we first came in here we thought there might be a cloakroom and a restroom, down that corridor over there," and before she can offer to accompany her, the little girl swivels around and, running, disappears into the hallway not far from the series of doors.

Instead of going after her as I had expected, Diane nods towards me. "You should come over here and take a look at this," she says, and when I arrive by her side, she tells me to open a door. I try one of the handles, and it is as unyielding as if the door, rather than being locked or chained, had been soldered to its frame. And then, like the man at my feet had done before, I shove hard against it. The entire wall shivers, and I smile at the curious thought that the doors had been painted or sculpted in place, a trompe l'oeil work of art, and that only the handles are real.

The man at my feet is now looking down the corridor into which his daughter has vanished, and with a groan he shifts slightly, as if he has finally decided to rise and follow her. But before he can get up, she reappears and runs haltingly toward us.

"There's nothing there," she says. "Just empty walls like everywhere else." She begins to whimper and fall to her knees, and her father wraps one arm around her shoulders as she buries her face into his shirt.

"Listen," says Diane, opening her purse and removing her phone. "It looks like you two could use some help. I've got the number of the front office on my phone, and maybe they can send somebody over here with water or first aid or whatever else you need." But after punching several numbers into the phone and raising it to her ear, she twists her mouth and shakes her head. "Damn," she says. "Damn!"

The man, a weak smile on his face, shifts again, and with his other hand withdraws his phone from his pants pocket, offering it to Diane. "You can use my phone," he says, "that is, if you prefer the silence of a dead battery to raw static."

"Well," I tell Diane, "after all, we are inside a mountain...."

She turns her eyes to me, silently, pleadingly, as if there is something I can do to help.

"I think we can probably catch up with the last tour group if we hurry," I say. "It wasn't so long ago that the line extended all the way down the wall, and there's sure to still be some staff inside." And then I add, addressing the father and his daughter. "We'll send someone back here to get you some help, or to find a quick way out for you... Unless, of course, you want to come along with us?"

"You mean in there?" he asks, and then reading from the inscription overarching the entryway to the tunnel, "Into the 'Theater of Eternal Delight?'"

"Wait a minute," says Diane, "Is that...?"

I put my finger to my lips, cautioning her. "Do you want to come with us?"

"No," he says. "We'll wait for you to send back some help. We'll depend on you for that," and turning his face away from me, he leans his cheek against the top of his child's head. As we turn from them, huddled on the floor, I notice a brackish puddle gradually seeping around the circumference of their knees.

"Are you completely sure..." Diane begins to ask, but probably recognizing our lack of choices, she never completes her question, and taking my arm, she joins me as we step inside the Theater of Eternal Delight.

EVERYTHING IS A MIRACLE

*Everything is a miracle. It is a miracle that one does not
dissolve in one's bath like a lump of sugar.*
- Pablo Picasso

When he grabbed the doorknob to open the door and leave for work, it would not turn. Perhaps his grip had been too loose, but when he applied more pressure, his hand slipped around the knob's surface as if it had been polished to a resistant-free sheen or covered with a transparent powder as slippery as grease. He pressed down hard with both hands, leveraging his weight against it, but it was still difficult to grasp and remained stationary while his hands slid around it. He simply did not have enough strength, he concluded, to turn the knob to his own door.

He was about to dry his palms, now moist with sweat, against the flanks of his jacket, but he hesitated, realizing that he was wearing his best suit. "Why am I wearing my best suit today?" he wondered, and then he thought, "I don't even remember bringing it home from the cleaners." Nor could he remember matching it with his only silk tie or this faded beige shirt that he hadn't worn in years, and never with this suit. Or remember brushing his teeth or even awakening to the buzz of his alarm and shutting it off.

Of course, he had settled into a morning routine for some time—particularly these last few months when he had been having such trouble sleeping—and his activities, from washing his face to lathering his cheeks to knotting his tie, he performed mechanically with little or no intervening thought. In fact, if a new tube of toothpaste or bar of soap were needed, he placed it on his bathroom shelf the night before, unboxed or unwrapped. The clothes he'd be wearing, he'd usually hang outside his closet, ready to be slipped into the next morning without a single thought.

But why was he wearing his best suit as well as his patent leather dress shoes? He shivered at the thought that his short-term memory might be leaving him, as it had his mother when she was only a few years older than his present age.

Her memory loss had been associated with a deep depression, eventually leading to severe dementia that forced her into a nursing home. But even though he had been subject to occasional fits of melancholy, they had never immobilized him as they had her. And even if the sudden onset of some mental incapacity explained his failure to remember how he had reached the threshold of his own door that morning, it did not explain the failure of the knob to turn and the door to open. What, after all, was to be done about that?

Moreover, where was Guinevere? His cat, too, was a creature of habit, and if he ever failed to set his alarm the night before, Guinevere would quickly rectify that oversight, since she expected to be fed the moment he arose from bed, even before he had dressed. But he had no recollection of putting on his bathrobe and coming downstairs to open a new can or of filling her bowl with fresh water, which she also demanded every morning. And if he had neglected to feed her, why was she not rubbing her head up against his ankles at that very moment?

She was nowhere to be seen. But again, no matter, since he still was not about to leave his condo until he found some way to open the door.

He recalled having had a problem with a stiff doorknob once before, and on that occasion, he had only to loosen the small screw on the stem of the knob for it to function smoothly. So for the moment, the solution to his problem was reduced to finding a Phillips head screwdriver that would fit the job, and he turned back to the long wardrobe closet beneath the staircase where his tools were stored on the shelves behind his winter overcoats.

The closet was open, but before entering he shoved a chair against its door, suddenly fearful that it might inadvertently swing shut behind him, and what if he had a similar problem with the closet doorknob once he was inside?

He swung his arm back and forth inside the closet in search of the string that hung from the bulb above his head, but he touched only emptiness. "Probably stuck on a clothes rack again," he thought, but no matter, since even in the darkness he was certain he could find a screwdriver, and slipping through his overcoats, he leaned forward, sliding his hand over the shelves behind. But then he stopped, suddenly sensing he was not alone inside the closet. He thought he heard a low, steady hiss, as if gas were escaping through a defective valve.

"Guinevere, is that you back there?" And as he peered into the blackness in the space behind the shelves, he thought he spied two hazel-green pinpoints of light.

"Gwenny, come out of there." The pinpoints of light vanished, as if they had turned and retreated deeper into the shadows of the closet.

"Gwenny?" he repeated in a softer, less threatening tone, and then he shrugged his shoulders, and rather than search further for his toolbox or his cat, he straightened up, since he was now gripping the handle of a small screwdriver. Had he swept it up unknowingly as he slid his hand blindly along the shelves? In any case, from its heft, it felt like the right size, and he backed out of the closet, back into the foyer to see if it would fit into the head of the screw he needed to adjust.

The tip of the shaft slipped easily but loosely into the notches, and at first the screw would not budge. But when he shifted his weight fully against the handle and twisted hard, the screw broke at once from its seal, spun around, and flew from its hole and off the screwdriver's tip to tumble down to the hardwood floor and, still spinning, roll beneath the door and into the hallway, outside.

"Well, I'd better hunt for that before going to work," he thought, and he turned the knob. It now spun easily without any resistance at all but, apparently, without any contact whatsoever with the latch. He turned it in the other direction, and it spun around just as loosely. The door remained closed.

"I need a cup of coffee," he thought. He would make a strong cup of coffee, take it with him into the living room, sit down on the couch, sip it slowly, and start the day over again. All that would be lacking was the morning paper, which, presumably, was waiting for him on the other side of the closed door, in the hallway. "Yes, a nice, leisurely cup of coffee," he said aloud, and he turned into the kitchen. He would now be late for work, but his department director was out of town at a conference and his staff could function quite competently, at least for several hours, in his absence.

He would have preferred a cappuccino, but grinding the coffee and preparing all the components would have been far too complicated in his current state of mind. In fact, even though his Braun coffeemaker had been cleaned and adjusted only a few months before, he hadn't used it since Laura, who made a cappuccino for both of them almost every weekday morning before leaving for work, had left him.

A cup of instant would do just as well, and when he lifted the teakettle and found it already to be filled with water, he placed it on the burner. But when he turned the knob on the stove, there was no flame, and the knob turned as loosely as the one on the door, swiveling around without restraint, as if connected to nothing. He could not detect the odor of gas but balanced the knob back into its "off" position anyway. "I suppose it's better not to be able to turn the gas on than not to be able to turn the gas off," he thought and wondered why nobody in maintenance had warned him that the gas in the building was being shut off that day, if that indeed was the case.

He had a similar thought when he tried to turn on the faucet for a glass of water and found the handle there to be just as slack as the one on the stove. When he reversed it to turn it off, it continued to revolve without any traction, as if the threads within its socket had been worn smooth. "Well, I'd better make sure the water to the sink's cut off, in case it comes back on," he thought, but when he looked inside the cabinet beneath the sink, he saw several pipes leading upward, each with a pair of valves, and he had no idea which of them needed to be adjusted. Before he could begin experimenting, he felt dizzy and unbalanced, and he needed to stand upright again. Reluctant to drop down on all fours and crawl into the tight, dark space beneath the sink in search of the right valves to turn—which, considering his recent experience with similar instruments, might not respond to his effort anyway—he hurried out of the kitchen, his head still not entirely clear.

"I'm going to really start over, right now," he said aloud, and wondering if he had inadvertently stumbled into some kind of nightmare, and feeling suddenly weak, as if his body had been drained at once of all energy, he decided to return to bed and try to go back to sleep. Once he had reawakened, even after only a short nap, perhaps things would have sorted themselves out, or at the very least, he would awake somewhat refreshed and not feel as if he had been sleepwalking through the morning, unequipped to deal with the obstacles thrown so arbitrarily across his path.

He climbed back up the stairs of his duplex into the master

bedroom.

The bed had been made, although there were soft indentations and wrinkles in the blanket, as if someone had slept lightly on top of it, without much movement, the night before. "Maybe that explains it," he thought. "I didn't remember changing into these clothes this morning because I never took them off last night." And although the suit he was wearing seemed to have been recently ironed as if he had just put it on fresh from the dry cleaner, this would not have been the first time he had collapsed into sleep on top of his covers without remembering, upon awakening, where he had been or what he had been doing just a few hours before. "Simply not enough sleep," he thought. "A little more sleep, that's all I need." Although he also would have appreciated a warm shower or bath to clear his head and steady his nerves before settling beneath the covers, and he regretted again that the water in his building had, apparently, been shut off.

But he realized that the idea of a bath had come to him because of the thick aroma of warm moisture in the air, as if Laura had just finished one of her long showers, and, a towel wrapped loosely about her body, she had opened the bathroom door to release a cloud of humidity into the bedroom as she shook her luxurious black hair and dried it vigorously before joining him in bed.

The bathroom door was ajar. He pushed it open to find the bathtub filled with water almost to the top. Approaching it, he swept his fingers across the surface, and it was still warm. "It must have been scalding hot when I filled it," he thought, and then he assumed he had completely forgotten about the bath as he tried to drive the drowsiness from his brain earlier that morning and, already completely dressed, had simply headed down the stairs to go to work.

But now even the thought of a leisurely soak invigorated him, and he would settle into the tub for as long as it took to clear his head and decide what to do, even if the water turned cool and then frigid as he lay there. He would not wait a moment longer. But when he lifted his hands to unknot his tie and begin to disrobe, he realized he was still holding the handle of the screwdriver in his left hand, and when he put it down on the sink, he saw that it was not the Phillips head screwdriver he had taken from the closet, but rather the six-inch boning knife he used to filet fish and bone chickens. It balanced uneasily on the sloping edge of the sink, swaying slightly up and down, and he picked it up again, wondering if he had unknowingly deposited the screwdriver in the cutlery drawer when he was in the kitchen and just as unknowingly retrieved the knife in its place. Preferring not to think about it, he lodged the knife inside the soap dish at the head of the tub, where it would be safe from falling to the tile floor and perhaps blunting or chipping its razor-sharp edge.

He then began to disrobe, and when he had finished, he laid his clothes just outside the bathroom door, suit, shirt, tie, underwear, all crumpled together. He did not intend to wear those garments again that day.

The bathroom door closed behind him and the latch snapped shut. He preferred not to test the door to see if it would open again but stepped directly into the tub where the lukewarm water wrapped itself softly around his shins as if welcoming him into its realm. He lowered himself slowly, breaking the surface tension with the backs of his thighs, and then stopped, gripping the edges of the tub with both hands and stiffening his arms, holding himself poised as if uncertain, reluctant to immerse his torso further into the water. But then he loosened his hold and continued his descent, releasing his grip when he finally touched bottom. Leaning back against the sloped head of the tub, he relaxed even more and began to slide deeper and deeper into the water that embraced his chest and then his shoulders and circled his neck and then his chin. He shut his eyes, and he continued to sink downward until the water covered his mouth, his nose, touched his eyelids, and closed over his head.

He refused to resist but continued to slide along the slippery porcelain bottom as if caught in the powerful undertow of a receding tide, as if the water was suddenly draining and he was being drawn along with it, spiraling downward into a funnel. The current strengthened, consuming him, and now he was afraid, but the pull was too strong, the pressure too heavy, and there was nothing he could grab on to, no traction, as he sunk downward with accelerating speed, eyes still tightly shut against the water, feeling nothing, thinking nothing, knowing only that he would be leaving behind nothing more than a clean white surface, smooth, lucent, dry, impenetrable.

INGRATITUDE

Just as I was opening her suitcase, she called up to me. "Could you please hurry up and bring my suitcase down, please."

"Sure," I said, "just give me a minute." But first I had to inspect its contents as it lay there flat on the bed, primarily to see if she had consulted my checklist before packing. After so many trips, for both business and pleasure, I considered my checklist to be an invaluable and necessary tool for travel preparation. She hadn't asked me for it, but she knew where it was, easily accessible in my desk drawer, top-right, along with my passport, the Xeroxed copy of my passport, and an envelope full of spare Euros.

I saw at once that she had followed most of my usual packing strategies, rolling up rather than folding her color-coordinated clothes, stuffing socks into shoes, compartmentalizing her underwear, and so forth. A quick count of her blouses, sweaters, and slacks informed me that she had packed light, as I had always advised. But the empty vacuum-seal plastic bags beneath her cosmetic kit were not part of my list—although perhaps they should have been—and where was the portable alarm clock and the international adapter? The former would ease her mind given the unreliability of those early morning wake-up calls, and the adapter she would surely need. Perhaps they were in her carry-on, but probably not. I closed the suitcase, zipping it shut.

"Will you hurry up? I don't want to be late!"

"Of course not," I muttered to myself. "Mustn't be late." Always we had to be at the airport hours in advance, even before 9/11 when interminable security lines became another obstacle for her to worry about, along with the possibility of flat tires on the freeway and suicides on the train lines. So, we would spend hours in an airport lounge or at a gate waiting for a plane to board, and the earlier we got there, it always seemed, the later our flight was sure to be delayed.

But it was always easier to tolerate Kathryn's insecurities than to risk a descent into hysteria, so I grabbed her suitcase and quickly hurried downstairs, where she was waiting for me by the front door, rummaging again through her purse to make sure she had the boarding pass she had printed out the night before.

"You sure you've got everything?" I said, setting the suitcase down next to her valise. "You want to go through your purse again?"

"I can only check and re-check so many times. I can't think of anything I might have forgotten, and as you always remind me, I can always buy missing stuff once I get there."

"Is your flight still on schedule?"

"I checked about fifteen minutes ago. Should I look again?"

"No."

"Ok, let's go."

"You know, you'll be there, like, hours…"

"I'd rather be there with plenty of time to spare than risk… You know how I am."

"Right, I know how you are. You're sure you want to go through with this?"

"I don't want to talk about it anymore. My mind's made up. I've got to start doing things on my own. I've been dependent on everyone else for too long. You never know when…"

"Okay, let's go." There was no point to discussing it with her any further. Clearly, she was determined to set out on her own.

In the past, Kathryn had always depended on me for most things. Of course, since I am, or at least had been before retirement, a certified public accountant, it was only natural that I manage most of our financial matters, whether it was the structuring of budgets, the handling of major purchases—our condo, car lease, and the like—our investments, retirement planning, and so forth. After all, I regularly had to deal with the intricate and often sloppy affairs of clients who were frequently careless and, on occasion, unscrupulous, whereas Kathryn, a professional copyeditor, rarely had to deal with anything more troubling or unruly than a mixed metaphor or a dangling participle. Moreover, as she told me so herself many times, Kathryn was quite content to leave most of these decisions up to me.

And never more so than when we were planning our vacations.

The season and duration, the destination, the lodgings, the everyday itinerary, and just about everything else was all up to me, and perhaps what Kathryn considered to be her "dependence" had all stemmed from that first trip we took together so many years ago.

Work obligations had forced us to postpone any thoughts about a honeymoon, and it wasn't until Kathryn had sufficiently recovered from her miscarriage, almost a year after the wedding, that I proposed a ten-day European vacation, something that I hoped would also help to restore her spirits along with her physical health. We didn't have much money then, but my parents offered support, and since Kathryn had recently completed her master's thesis on Jacobean drama, I thought a trip to England would be just the right thing to reinvigorate a marriage that had, frankly, gotten off to a rocky start.

I had planned a good deal of theater, a diet of fish and chips, and a pub crawl or two, but when our flight was cancelled at the airport, all my planning was thrown into disarray. We flew out on the following morning, but we arrived on a Bank Holiday, making it difficult to exchange the traveler's checks I had brought along as our major source of currency. Fortunately, a fellow passenger took pity on us and offered to drive us from Heathrow into the city, dropping us off in front of our B&B. But when we reached the front desk, the owner of Peterborough House informed us that our reservation had been canceled. Upon hearing this, Kathryn became even more agitated, but her anxiety had helped us get that ride into the city, and I thought her condition might again be an asset as I stubbornly continued to argue, vehemently, with the proprietor. But when she finally threatened to call the police if we did not vacate the premises immediately, I withdrew back into the hallway, where Kathryn had earlier retreated, only to find that she had disappeared.

I suppose it was fortunate that the police had already been called, since a simple matter of a commercial dispute had now escalated into a case of a missing person. In fact, Kathryn was gone for almost two days before I was called up to a constabulary near Hampstead Heath, where she had been found wandering and disoriented. Tired, hungry, and a bit dehydrated, she was still in relatively good physical shape, but her purse, along with her wallet, was gone. Fortunately, she still had her passport, and although the police questioned her thoroughly, neither they nor I could discover anything about what had happened during those two days. She simply could not, or would not, remember anything, and since there was no complaint or any sign of criminal activity, we were soon free to go. We returned home as quickly as possible.

Naturally, Kathryn was reluctant to travel for some time, especially overseas, and we both used our increasing workloads as an excuse to avoid dealing with her fears. But eventually I managed to convince her to join me on short overnight road trips—Madison, Wisconsin and Galena, Illinois—so long as I took the car in for maintenance before setting out and handled all the arrangements myself. She would follow along, as if she had no say in the matter, like a hostage rather than a companion, and even though at the end of the trip she said she had enjoyed herself, she never ceased to remind me that the best part was the return home. A few more years, and I managed to get her on a plane, once to D.C. and then to San Francisco, and finally to those European cities I always wanted to see: Paris, Vienna, Rome.

Of course, I was responsible for planning every passing minute of the trip, from the hotels we stayed at, to the restaurants we ate in, to the sites we saw, and the transportation we took. I suppose it would have been easier to book tours and let commercial outfits and professional guides handle all the troublesome details. But I always wanted to travel independently, making my own choices, and although the responsibilities were often challenging, my labor was usually rewarded with pleasant and memorable experiences, and believe me, I took considerable pride in the success of most of our European vacations. I only regretted that Kathryn rarely acknowledged all the effort and care required for such constantly good results. And, of course, on those few occasions when unforeseen circumstances derailed my best intentions, all the blame for any discomfort and the burden of finding solutions fell on my shoulders.

Once when our connecting flight was canceled at JFK, I was the one responsible for finding overnight accommodations amid all those "no vacancies" and for fighting our way onto the following morning's flight to Milan, and I have no doubt she blamed me and only me for that dreary motel room where we spent a sleepless night. And when she was careless enough to have her purse stolen in Brussels, I was the one who spent hours filling out police reports, cancelling credit cards, arranging for passport photos, and reserving an appointment at the consulate while she stood aside, shaking and in tears, waiting for me to sort everything out or for something else to go wrong.

But on both occasions, I persevered, and everything turned out all right in the end, and we returned home with bags, cameras, and memories full of souvenirs.

So, needless to say, it came as a shock to me when Kathryn, a few months after she followed me into retirement, informed me that she wanted to take an overseas trip by herself, alone and independent, without any assistance from me, as if all those vacations we had enjoyed together, all those hours of meticulous planning, all that labor and effort I had sacrificed for our mutual benefit had meant nothing to her.

My complete surprise was followed by my complete silence, which I suppose she took for my approval, since by the end of the week she had already found a destination.

"Prague? Why Prague?" I asked.

"I don't know. Of all the European cities we visited, I guess I felt most comfortable in Prague."

As far as I was concerned, Prague had been one of my least enjoyable experiences, largely because our hotel was too close to the Charles Bridge, and we were overwhelmed by swarms of tourists whenever we ventured outside. It seemed that every restaurant, café, and bar we visited was packed full of Americans and Brits, and maybe that was what made Kathryn feel so comfortable there.

"And besides," she said, "everyone seemed to speak English."

"Once you're out of the center that may no longer be the case. If you're looking for English speakers, why not the UK? Why not London?"

"No," she replied firmly, and then she informed me that there was no point in suggesting alternatives since she had already made all the arrangements.

"Really? For when?"

"The end of the month. Two weeks from today."

"That's Easter weekend, you know."

"I know, and they take Easter very seriously in Prague. There'll be festivals and fairs."

"And crowds. Lots of crowds."

"Tell me about it! Almost everything was booked up. But I found a nice small hotel. Here."

She handed me a printout from the Hotel U Vyšehrad.

"That's for you. I've written out the dates on the top."

"Vyšehrad? That's not in the center of town."

"I've booked a limousine service. They'll take me directly there from the airport." She handed me another printout. "They'll meet me at the arrival gate with one of those little posters with your name printed on it. I've made everything as simple as possible, and the hotel's close to a subway stop. Remember, we used the subway a couple of times when we were there."

I remembered, and I remembered how difficult it was to understand the announced stations from the loudspeaker inside the train: Staroměstská, Malostranská, Hradčanská. Kathryn never knew it, but we missed our intended stop twice, once forcing a long walk back to a restaurant and once requiring a taxicab to get us out of a dark and seedy residential district.

"And this will only be a pilot run. Now that I've retired, I might want to travel a little more. The Taj Mahal, Angkor Wat. I've always wanted to see Asia. So different from all those stodgy European cities."

"Europe's about as far as I can fly. You know, my back can only take…"

"I know. That's why it's important for me to become accustomed to traveling on my own."

She asked nothing more of me than on her day of departure to drive her to the Blue Line on her way to O'Hare.

After pulling up at one of the stations on Dearborn, I removed her suitcase and valise from the trunk and deposited them in front of the elevator on the street.

"You know, I didn't care very much for Prague," I said, "but I would have agreed to go with you if you had asked."

"But then what would have been the point? You always handled everything, and everything seemed so easy for you. Not the least bit of trouble or worry. I've got to learn to do these things on my own, and so far, I think I've done a pretty good job of it, thank you. Moreover, I'm eager to confront any obstacles that might come my way. It'll be a good experience. The Great Unknown. You should be proud of me."

I leaned over to kiss her on the cheek. "Bon voyage."

"And don't forget to water the plants. Every day."

It was still fairly early in the afternoon, and since the streets were relatively free of traffic, I arrived quickly back home. But I waited several hours until I was sure Kathryn's flight was in the air, and, after watering the plants, I emailed the limousine service to cancel her airport pick-up. The Hotel U Vyšehrad I called directly to inform them that my wife had been forced to postpone her visit to Prague at the very last minute and that her reservation would need to be canceled. The manager assured me that since there was a waiting list there would be no problem in booking the room and probably no reason to forfeit our deposit, which was usually the case.

I didn't cancel her two credit cards but requested only that they be put on hold and frozen. Kathryn had decided to take a considerable amount of currency in Euros along with her, quite enough, in fact, for her to purchase a return ticket home, and all things considered, returning immediately back home would have been a quick and easy solution, the reasonable thing for her to do.

But, unfortunately, that's not what happened.

TO DAVID, ON DEATH ROW

August 1, 1992

Dear David,
The week before you killed her, your mother wrote to tell me I was your father. Of course, I didn't believe her then and I still don't now. It had been nearly twenty years since we last spoke, and surely, I would have heard from her before if she really thought that was the case. So, I assumed—although she said nothing about it in her letter—that your mother was experiencing hard times and that I would be hearing from her soon about money. With that in mind, I don't know if I ever would have replied to her, but, of course, your subsequent action made any attempt at communication on my part pointless.

But now that you have decided to end all appeals and your date is fast approaching, I thought I would write to you. I don't know what Carol may have told you about me, if anything, but I nevertheless feel that your mother's letter has obligated me to tell you something about our time together, for what it was worth.

Carol and I knew each other for only a short period, maybe three months. I can't remember the exact length or dates, since it was so long ago, and when it was over, it was over for good.

We first met in a hardware store. I was a graduate student then and unaccustomed to approaching women whom I didn't know. But I was lonely, your mother was quite attractive, and she seemed to welcome my attentions. After a few nervous exchanges, I remember having done most of the talking, but Carol did seem interested in what I had to say about lighting fixtures and then about books when we later adjourned to a bar. Afterwards we went to my apartment and did not emerge from my bedroom until the next morning.

That first encounter came as quite a surprise to me, since I was never very adept with women—the sexual revolution of the late sixties had pretty much passed me by—and I felt more like an observer of a scene rather than one of its principal actors. Your mother later told me that, according to her therapist, she had at the time been "borderline catatonic," which may have accounted for my uncharacteristic success.

And, in case you think I was taking advantage of her, she also told me that her therapist thought I was good for her and helpful in alleviating what she diagnosed to be a severe and dangerous case of depression. Initially, of course, I had no idea that Carol was even under the care of a doctor and, as I later came to realize, in those first days I was probably seeing her at her best.

But opposites attract, and for a short time, we were infatuated with each other (although let me assure you that despite my exuberant passion for Carol, I always made certain to take every precaution). As I'm sure you know, your mother was from Kentucky, and her background and many social contacts with the Appalachian community at that time in Chicago's Uptown neighborhood were fascinating to me. She, in turn, seemed intrigued by my urban-Jewish roots and, at least for a time, pretended to be interested in my literary pursuits. But it wasn't long before she tried to involve me in her friends' political protests, which I resisted, particularly after one such demonstration—over rent control, I think—became violent and led to several arrests. For her part, she failed to see any value in my study of Robert Louis Stevenson's prosody, especially when considered against the oppression of her people and the ravages of strip mining. In fact, her contempt for my work eventually led to the incineration of the third chapter of my thesis. Fortunately, I had retained earlier drafts, and Carol did apologize, but we both suspected—and we were right—that it was over by then. I'll spare you the uglier details, but I believe our last date encapsulates our relationship in its final decadent stage.

It was my birthday, and I think we both wanted to give it one last shot. Carol had invited me for dinner, and I had arranged for tickets to a blues concert to follow. She had just quarreled with her roommate, so for the first time we would be alone for the night in her apartment. Carol was not a particularly skilled cook, but she knew how to follow a recipe, and I concluded from the grimy pots and pans heaped in the kitchen sink, she had spent a large part of the day over the stove. And it was good, too, although quite rich—smothered pork chops, I remember, corn pudding, a pecan pie—and unfortunately, it did not agree with me. In fact, I'm afraid I deposited a good part of what I had eaten in an alleyway next to the blues club. When we returned to her apartment, she invited me in, but I declined, telling her that I was still not feeling well. She replied by calling me a pig. "I expected as much," she said, and when I protested and told her I was sick, she said, "That's right, any excuse to leave me with all those goddamned dishes. What else could I expect from a pig like you." Her reaction came as quite a surprise to me, since I was her guest, this was my birthday, and I can't remember how many times I cleaned up my own kitchen by myself after a breakfast with her or a dinner from the night before.

Yet I didn't want it all to end on that sour note, and I intended to call her the following day. But when I opened my door to retrieve the morning paper—still with a splitting headache and an upset stomach—I was confronted with a huge black garbage bag swollen and filled to the brim with shards, splinters, and other fragments—stained with clotted sauces and coagulated fats—from what was left of the plates, saucers, and glasses from the previous night. The contents had spilled over into the hallway, scattered there for me to clean up before the neighbors awoke and complained. It didn't help matters any that the jagged edge of one porcelain dish sliced deeply into my palm, a wound that became infected and cost me the use of my right thumb to this day! Of course, I was furious, and I have no idea what I might have done if I ran into Carol at that moment. I'm not a violent person, but... well...

And so, I truly believed you and sympathized with you when you testified in your defense about the cigarette burns, the electric cables, the discipline closet, her abusive boyfriends, and your poor little dog. (In fact, I strongly suspected, from some words and actions recollected after the fact, that my own cat at the time—an affectionate tabby named Melody—would not have survived a relationship with Carol had it lasted much longer.) And even if the jury did not believe all your stories or, if they did, did not feel they justified your lethal response, particularly considering the way you chose to carry it out, I have no doubt from my own experience with your mother you were speaking the truth and suffered greatly from it. I understand perfectly the provocation and the sudden intensity of your emotions and your blind rage, and I could not pretend that

I would have acted any differently if I had been in your place.

And again, for what it's worth, I commend your decision to end all appeals, and I recognize in that a considerable sense of responsibility and honest self-respect.

Feel free to answer this letter, but I want you to know that I will make no further attempt to contact you. I also would have no objection to meeting with you, but I doubt that it would be possible under these circumstances, unless I decided to declare myself, which I have no reason for nor intention of doing. It would take more than Carol's word to persuade me that you and I had any more in common than a mutual although intimate acquaintance with a disturbed woman who can no longer speak for herself.

With that in mind, I want you to know that my thoughts go out to you, and may God be with you.

Sincerely,
J.T. Altheimer

THE COLONIZERS

Day One

The society we encountered is a primitive one, according to Dr. Stroxa, yet one that is highly structured and regulated. She had also reported that our initial contact would likely be peaceful and that the inhabitants would probably not respond with violence unless provoked.

Dr. Stroxa proved to be correct. There was no resistance.

In fact, hardly any notice at all was taken of our arrival—a curious lack of interest, particularly in view of our spectacular entrance.

We had intended to land on a flat, grassy plain some five hundred meters from the nearest settlement. But a sudden upsurge in wind velocity pushed us off our trajectory, and we impacted on a field of ripe grain, ready for harvest.

Half the crops were incinerated by our afterburners. Yet the agricultural workers nearby seemed undisturbed by the destruction we had caused. No astonishment, no alarm, hardly any interest whatsoever. They simply ceased work, drew near, observed us as we disembarked, and then resumed their tasks, as if the appearance of an alien force in their midst were an everyday occurrence.

Nor have they made any attempt to communicate with us, and I suspect that it will be some time before we establish contact from our side. In fact, as far as I can tell, it seems that the inhabitants of this planet have no language at all, at least not an oral one.

Yet how can this be? In all our data banks, there is no record of any intelligent lifeform having developed a structured society without the benefit of a language of some sort. Of course, we now may be dealing with one of the lower orders, and Stroxa has suggested that language might be the privilege of a ruling class not yet contacted. But such a cultural monopoly is also without precedence.

They could, of course, be telepaths. But Arno and Reva are qualified telepaths, and neither senses any unusual stimulation. I have nevertheless directed Arno to observe their activities closely. Perhaps he will eventually break through their seemingly impenetrable indifference.

Or could they be androids? Dr. Lemy assures me that they are completely organic with physiologies similar to our own. Yet their activities are so fragmented and mechanical, they could easily be taken for robots. Dr. Lemy suggested the possibility of organic androids, but he and I both know that previous experiments of that kind have all been failures.

In any case, Lemy is eager for a dissection. I've warned him that a specimen must come to him by natural means or not at all. There must be no provocation.

In the meantime, we shall concentrate on securing our base compound. Research strategies must also be established, and our biological surveys must begin at once. Fortunately, it appears that our operations will not be opposed by the population.

I have reminded the team that there is far more glory in a peaceful, bloodless colonization than in one accomplished through violence. The spoils belong to us no matter what the means, and although I've cautioned them against overconfidence, it seems likely that our operation will run smoothly—as routine as the pacification of the Orion system.

Preliminary Observations

The atmosphere is well oxygenated, quite invigorating, in fact. The soil is rich, highly nitrogenous. It will support whatever vegetation we choose to transplant. Already I'm leaning toward recommending a second-level agricultural colony with a minimum of both creative demolition and technological and military support.

The cataloguing and evaluations have proceeded without complications. Lemy complains that, apart from those planets ravaged by thermonuclear war, he has never seen an environment with such a scarcity of diverse vegetable and animal material. He and Stroxa have already been on numerous excursions and have been able to identify only a few grasses, a single flowering plant, and one grain that the inhabitants cultivate.

There are woodlands, but these seem to be orchards rather than forests. They consist of only two varieties of conifer, probably the male and female version of the same tree. The female produces a sweet nut, rich in protein and a staple in the diets of the inhabitants.

There is insect life: an ant, a bee, a moth, an earthworm. I use the singular intentionally, since there seems to be no variation within a species, as if the evolutionary competition has been so fierce that there could be only one survivor within an ecological niche.

So far, we have discovered no intermediate stages between these few insects and the humanoid population, leading me to suspect that either all life on this planet was recently imported or that all intermediate animal forms have been exterminated, artificially or naturally.

Drs. Lemy and Stroxa begin exploration of the southern latitudes tomorrow, and perhaps they will be able to account for these curious gaps.

The Agricoles

We have come no nearer to understanding the forces that control and motivate the native populations. They continue to remain as inaccessible to us as a colony of bacteria. It's very discouraging. Even the most primitive Neoliths maintain symbol systems that can be interpreted and used. But these villagers behave like a community of mute reptiles, incapable of conscious thought!

Yet their society is strangely regulated. Their customs and activities are more rigidly defined than any described in the data banks. Far more regimented than even the totalitarian systems of the Gamma network, which, to the eternal gratitude of the entire universe, we have forever eradicated!

Reva refers to them as "agricoles," for their existence revolves around cultivation. Hoeing, weeding, irrigating, pruning, mulching, fertilizing; and although these are complex tasks, all their movements are highly formalized, as if each activity had been broken down into its separate components and programmed into their brains. Even a sophisticate from the home territories could learn and accomplish every task for farming a plot of land simply by watching them work for a few days.

Is this how they communicate, how they transfer knowledge over generations, through formalized patterns of movements? Or are their actions instinctual, like the mating habits of birds or the dancing of bees?

On the other hand, all our computer simulations define this society as a hierarchical one, with structure imposed from the top. Yet we have found no trace of dominion, or central power, or traditional imperatives, or even religious authority. Could it be that a superior race "domesticated" the current inhabitants, and then either abandoned them or were themselves extinguished like the intermediate animals? If so, we have yet to uncover any traces of a superior civilization, although we could be dealing with a population that vanished millennia ago.

I shall recommend that a paleo-archaeologist be assigned to the colony, as well as a professional ethnographer.

Specimens

Stroxa disagrees with me. She insists that a research grantee at the cadet level would be quite adequate. "This planet is hardly worth a baccalaureate thesis!" she insists. "To waste the time of a fully accredited ethnographer would be scandalous. She'd kill herself out of boredom within the first year!"

She also feels that a paleo-archaeologist would be useless. In their entire exploration of the southern hemisphere, Stroxa and Lemy found no signs of a superior civilization. Nothing new, nothing different from what we had observed here. The same vegetation, the same insects, the same absence of higher forms of animal life.

The agricultural communities, too, are almost identical to those in the northern latitudes. The southerners subsist on the same limited diet of grain and nuts, wear the same brown tunics that have all the character of burlap sacks, use the same elementary utensils and tools, eat at the same troughs like livestock, and sleep in the same kind of communal barracks.

There is greater use of fire to compensate for the cooler climate, but in general the southern populations also exist without any meaning or variety in their lives beyond the tending of their staple crops.

"There is a society here," says Stroxa, "but no culture."

Already Stroxa and Lemy feel they have collected sufficient data for their report, and I have directed them to prepare for their return.

Specimens of all identifiable species of animal and vegetable life have been transferred to the biochambers, with the single exception of *Cattleya lemy*. This is the flower that grows in clusters sporadically at the fringes of the settlements. It seems to be a wild growth, although the agricoles spend as much time caring for these plants as for their crops, and whenever one of our expedition draws near, several villagers are sure to interpose their bodies between the visitor and the flower, preventing close inspection.

Lemy, however, managed to examine a specimen one morning shortly before dawn, when the agricoles were asleep.

"The fragrance is extraordinary for such a small flower," he reported, "and it drives the bees to delirium. The fact that the bees are nocturnal also accounts for the phosphorescence of the petals. Since its bloom is the single source of nectar and pollen for the bees, and since honey forms an essential ingredient for the agricoles' favorite beverage, I can understand the desire to protect the plant. It's an orchid and shall be named *Cattelya lemy*. I can acquire a specimen tomorrow without anyone being the wiser."

I informed the doctor that he would have to be satisfied with a photoscan. Under no circumstances would I permit him to remove one of the plants.

"But the Botanical Commission will never accept classification from a photoscan! They require a living specimen! There must be a dissection as well. Why, some colonial agricultural engineer will claim to have discovered the species, and it will be his name that appears in catalogues throughout the universe, not mine!"

I told the doctor that I had no interest whatsoever in the nomenclature of a plant. My directive was to avoid any confrontation that might jeopardize our mission and interfere with the establishment of the colony.

Apparently Lemy did not agree with me. He seemed quite upset by my decision.

The Burial

I was right about the orchid. It seems to have significant meaning for the agricoles and perhaps even plays a sacred role in their lives.

This evening while I was sweeping the outskirts of one of the settlements in search of buried artifacts, I noticed one of the workers wandering away from the fields. He was pressing his hands against his temples, and his mouth was wide open as if he wanted to cry out in pain.

And then he collapsed. Soon afterwards, his companions gathered around him, and with the same composure and indifference with which they performed all their tasks, they stripped the tunic from him, dragged him over to a nearby orchid, and scattered compost over his body.

A shallow grave was dug beneath the flower, and after wrapping the roots around his corpse, they buried him there.

For even the most primitive of societies, death and burial have religious significance. Does this orchid represent for the agricoles an afterlife, a resurrection? Can the simple ceremony I witnessed this evening help us understand this culture which so far has resisted all our efforts to penetrate its silence?

When I informed Lemy of the incident, he seemed more interested in the circumstances of the villager's death than in the details of the burial.

"An implant!" he exclaimed. "An implant in the brain! That's how they are controlled and monitored!"

"Perhaps," I replied. "But it could just as easily have been a natural death. A stroke of some sort."

"There's one way to find out," he muttered, and it was then that I should have confined him to quarters.

Exhumation

They dissected him, Lemy and Stroxa both, shortly before dawn as he lay there in his grave. There was no implant.

"They're very much like us," reported Lemy, "although I only had enough time and light for a cursory examination. Since those roots had enmeshed the entire body, I concentrated on the brain. Both hemispheres appear to be well developed, and I cannot account physiologically for the absence of language or a complex culture. The vocal cords, however, had atrophied, as if they had degenerated into vestigial organs like our appendix. The cause of death: a massive brain hemorrhage."

I did not thank Lemy for his information, and I'm sure he did not expect me to be grateful. On the other hand, there is no point in initiating punitive measures, although I certainly intend to report his insubordination to the Central Council. I ordered him to prepare for liftoff tomorrow.

"The sooner, the better," was his only reply, and despite his assurances that the desecration was unobserved, I have multiplied our guard for the night.

Parting Gifts

Today, on the morning of the command ship's departure, they made contact. Apparently, they sensed Lemy's covetous lust for their beloved orchids, for as soon as he emerged from his quarters, a pair of agricoles presented him with two young specimens, a supply of mulch, and a small colony of bees, their hive encased in a crude wooden box.

"The bees are necessary in nature for cross-pollination," explained Lemy. "But that can be performed by hand in the laboratory. These are immature plants. But even so, look at how the labellum glows with color. And the fragrance! It was almost stupefying last night. I can see why they've made a shrine of this flower, particularly in view of the overpowering monotony of this ecosystem."

I asked him if there were any additional attempts to communicate, other than the presentation of the gifts. He informed me that as soon as they dropped the objects at his feet, they retreated to the fields and resumed working.

"But they've given me all I need for successful cultivation. As you know, I'm an excellent gardener and even have a hybrid *Oncidium* to my credit. I wonder how long before they reach maturity. You should have seen the size of the one out there. The rhizome was as thick as your arm. No wonder they spend so much time tending to the base of the plant, aerating its roots. If only I had another specimen that I could dissect…"

I said that it was a pity he would not have the opportunity, and I helped him carry the orchids into the botanical chamber,

I was relieved to see them take off. Both Stroxa and Lemy have valuable minds, but I cannot tolerate insubordination. Moreover, they were becoming restless and unpredictable. It requires the patience and discipline of a soldier to bivouac on alien terrain for years, preparing it for colonization. Our scientists require challenges of far greater complexity than can be found on this dull planet.

The Attack

I suppose after half a year on this planet without incident, with hardly a variation in the daily routine, we had grown complacent. We were unprepared for the raid, especially one so well-conceived and coordinated. We were easily overpowered.

They destroyed everything, without emotion and as methodically as if they were clearing ground for a new field. Our equipment, our weapons, our databanks, our supplies, our communications are all gone. It will be months before the command vehicle even realizes that they have lost contact with us.

They harmed none of us, even though five of their own were killed and dozens wounded. When they finished their work of destruction, they left us as calmly as if they had just paid us a cordial social visit, carrying their dead and wounded along with them.

We have been completely neutralized, reduced to their level. We now must reassess our situation, determine what can be salvaged and what can be rebuilt, and then take defensive precautions to prevent such an outbreak from reoccurring.

I will persist in my observations. I want the colony to be well acquainted with their resources and challenges before it touches down in force. Naturally, as soon as the mission achieves orbit, I will request permission for retaliatory action.

Until then, we need only to survive.

Arno

Arno had been observing them for longer periods and at closer proximity than any of us.

He had yet to make contact, but he knew them as well as if he had been studying them under laboratory conditions. On occasion, he even joined in their activities, and I thought it would be easy for him to acquire farm implements for our compound. Some of our seed supplies escaped destruction. We could grow vegetables and be free of those abominable nuts.

I was therefore pleased when I saw him with a hoe, turning the soil with the others. Two hours later, he was still working in the fields. I asked Reva to investigate, to see if anything was wrong.

Reva had always been Arno's closest companion, but I still warned her to be careful. I suppose she felt Arno would never harm her. She didn't even flinch when, after she touched him on the shoulder, he swung around and split her skull with his hoe.

By the time I arrived, Arno had already removed her clothes, and the others were helping him drag her to one of the orchids. There was nothing I could do. The sharp edge of the hoe had cleft her forehead nearly in half. I watched as Arno and the others dug a trench at the base of the plant, working like surgeons with their hoes and picks, careful not to damage the bulbous rhizome or the roots.

After covering Reva's body with mulch, they shoved her into the hole, encircling her with a tangle of roots. As soon as the first tendril touched the blood from her skull, the entire plant quivered as though with greed and delight, and I suddenly understood everything.

After walking slowly back to the compound, I armed myself with a crowbar and waited for Arno to appear. He did not return, spending the night, I suppose, with them.

Of course, Arno is not to blame. Nor are the agricoles. It is neither he nor they whom I will confront tomorrow.

Confrontation

There was no point in approaching the orchids during the day. Their protectors were on the alert.

I chose the hour before dawn, traveling far to an outlying hillock. I was determined to destroy one with my own hands.

From my first day on the planet, I had been aware of the fragrance. Even from a distance, it pervaded the night air. I could detect a characteristic aroma, but the overall impression was never the same, varying in intensity and hue like the many shades of a primary color.

As I neared the flower, its perfume seemed to reflect the depth of my rage, thickening, becoming dense and heavy, enveloping me like a coagulating web that all my strength could not tear through.

When I was close enough to touch it and raised the crowbar above my head, my brain began to ring as if it were sounding an alarm, crying out in self-preservation, and the veins in my temples began to pound and boil. A fire had ignited inside my skull, and I can remember nothing else.

In the morning, there was dirt beneath my fingernails and in the crevices of my palms and on my pants around the kneecaps, as if I had spent all night kneeling at the base of the orchid, hoeing the ground with my hands, aerating its roots.

Survival of the Fittest

As an exercise in evolutionary biology, Dr. Lemy invariably asked his students to choose a lower form of life and, assuming the life form had acquired intelligence, extrapolate the civilization that would eventually be developed from it.

None of us cadets were ever foolish enough to select a rooted plant for an example. We all knew that Lemy held that root-bound plants, dominated by the circumstances of their environment, could never develop tools and would therefore never have the capacity to control nature and form a culture.

Lemy was wrong.

It seems that *Cattleya lemy* was somewhat ahead of its humanoid competitors in the development of intelligence. It may not have had the ability to create tools itself, but it was apparently quite capable of controlling the wills of those who could.

Now *Cattelya lemy* has decided to colonize, like us. I wonder if it will be as successful as it has been here. Dr. Lemy, as he reminded me, is a very good gardener, and he once told me that the seed capsule of a single orchid can contain over a million seeds.

AFLOAT

Let me be very clear about this: I did not agree to participate for my own sake. After twenty years of service as Chief Scientific Officer, I had much to offer to our government and to future generations, and although the expense was considerable, my experience, my technical expertise, my abilities to innovate and process information would certainly produce value far beyond the initial investment and the custodial costs, by tenfold, at least.

After all, genius—and that is not my own characterization but that of the media and my colleagues—is not a commodity that is easily obtained, but a gift to be appreciated and nurtured when it so infrequently appears.

Nor do I take personal credit for having defied, or at least temporarily deferred, death. As with most technological advances, this was the product of years of development, thousands of hours of work by hundreds of technicians, a series of timely synergies, and, since our stated objectives were of another sort altogether, not a little bit of serendipity and luck.

Let me explain. For many years it had been the charge of my division to develop an AI capacity that would equal the cognitive power of the human brain. Naturally, we modeled our efforts on the thing itself, although it was generally believed by most of our biotechnicians that any attempt to replicate the full functioning of the brain, with its hundred billion neurons connected by ten trillion synapses, was an exercise in futility. And who knows, perhaps they were right, since we never managed to achieve more than a crude imitation of the higher powers of cognition.

Along the way we were remarkably effective in converting visual and aural signals into electronic configurations, and it was those same skeptical biotechnicians who decided to apply these digital conversions to organic neural receptors, an essential component to the success of what was to follow. If we could, they argued, enable machines to "see" and "hear," then why not the blind and the deaf, too, and before long we had patented devices destined to enrich the lives of millions of disabled persons. Advances like these gave our group a solid reputation for biomedical innovation, and before long, the Saratoga Project was assigned to my division.

I had been monitoring Saratoga for some time, and I was impressed by its progress in preserving organs—hearts, livers, lungs, and the like—in isolation. But when the team came under my direction, I was astonished to learn that they had reached a stage where the health and viability of an isolated organ could be maintained, in a controlled environment, almost indefinitely. Of course, their goal was to inventory these organs for eventual transplantation, and until Saratoga became a part of my division, no one had seriously considered experimenting with the human brain. Just as we had failed to replicate its almost infinite complexity artificially, transplanting the brain would have required an equally advanced technology, far beyond our capacities at that time.

But simply preserving the brain in isolation seemed to be an attainable goal, and since, as any reputable philosopher would argue, personal identity resides in that organ, transferring a healthy brain into a secure, artificial environment would simplify the task of prolonging individual existence long after other organic functions had failed. Certainly, it was an experiment worth attempting, and the fact that my own cancer had by then been diagnosed and declared inoperable had little to do with this change in direction, although I don't deny that it may have hastened the process.

As I am trained as an engineer, I supervised the construction of the environment myself. Of course, it was far more complex than the devices that sustained hearts and lungs. But once the nutrient mix, the varying concentrations of proteins and enzymes, and the daily modifications in ionization levels were determined, the problem became one of implementation rather than content, and I saw to it that the resources were made available to create not only a functioning environment but one that would operate for at least as long as our civilization endured. The plutonium generator, for instance, would provide sufficient energy to keep the mechanism functioning for dozens of millennia. Huge, sealed vats were constructed to store the components for the supplies of glycogen, phosphates, lipids, and enzymes, the contents to be dispensed drop-by-drop into the solution where all the chemical reactions would occur. With much of the waste matter being recycled back into the system, healthy organic life could be sustained for almost as long as the generator produced the energy to keep the systems in operation. Heat displacement would eventually bring the whole apparatus to a halt, but my chief mathematician assured me that even without maintenance, stasis would not occur, theoretically, until long after the planet spun from its orbit and fell into the sun.

Of course, without the ability to communicate, as in to receive stimulation and respond in kind, I would neither have authorized nor participated in such a venture. By then our digital conversion biotechnologies had reached such a degree of sophistication that the most complex information could be easily communicated directly to the relevant centers of the brain. If my mental ability could be sustained and enriched by a continuous flow of intellectual stimulation, and if communications, in return, could be sent from this superior and continually expanding intelligence, contributing to the betterment of all posterity, then such an experiment would surely be worth the effort, regardless of the cost and the considerable sacrifice. On the other hand, if such communications were not successfully received, or if my own observations were not being transmitted, or if either of these activities became dysfunctional in the future, the experiment was to be immediately terminated, and I would be accorded the memorial rites due to an official of my standing and accomplishment.

Ordinarily, the surgery itself would have been a fearful thing to contemplate. But by then, my body had withered away before my eyes, an ugly, painful encumbrance requiring larger and larger dosages of analgesics, resulting in longer and longer periods of drugged stupor. Success or annihilation, I was prepared for either one, and even though all the systems had not been fully tested, I signed the releases, endowed all my worldly goods to the financing of the project, and instructed the Surgical Division to proceed with the intervention a month ahead of schedule.

The procedure took three days, and even though life support was a minor concern in comparison with the tedious implantation of the thousands of microelectrodes, I was later informed that I had been twice pronounced clinically dead, for periods of twenty seconds each.

Of course, I have no recollection of this, no more than a patient under anesthesia remembers the removal of an appendix. When I awoke, it was to a field of golden sunflowers—the test pattern I had chosen for the occasion—and when I received confirmation of my first transmission ("Mr. Watson, come here, I want you!"), I would have cried for joy if I'd had the tear ducts to do so.

I remained awake for several days, exploring my new environment. I had been born into another world, and like an infant I could first only crawl about, as it were, and take a few awkward steps. Tests had been arranged in advance, but they were far more rigorous than I'd anticipated, and when they were finally completed, I fell into a long, hallucinatory sleep. I awoke still exhausted, and I immediately induced another period of deep sleep, something I could accomplish with relative ease.

Before the operation and with the help of electrochemical stimuli, I had become adept at initiating trancelike states of sleep, full of pleasurable images and experiences. The most effective of these stimulants had been introduced into my environment, and I was gratified to discover that I not only could descend into these trances whenever I wished, but that I could usually manipulate the visions, acting as a director more or less of my own dreams. They were illusions, of course, but it was nevertheless a consolation to be able to experience the pleasures of the body—taste, touch, smell, even sex—as if I had been grafted back into the youthful and vigorous self that I'd thought had been lost to me forever. Even on those occasions when my visions would darken, as dreams often do, I could usually dispel the threatening shadows and escape back into a dream that was, if not ecstatic, at least safe.

Although I could manipulate these trances, I was often slow to wake from them, and my team was given strict instructions to arouse me after every eight-hour period of sleep. The schedule that I then adopted was similar to the one I'd followed before the operation. Upon awakening, I would be supplied with the latest scientific literature and technical findings, the most significant symposium papers and referred articles, and the general news of the day. Free of the conflicting diversions and interruptions of the body, I found that I could assimilate and retain a remarkable amount of data, but for no more than eight hours, after which I began to read the latest books, listen to the best music, experience whatever could be digitized and fed directly into my neural receptors. This second eight-hour period was primarily a time for relaxation and reflection, but it also contributed to the store of memories and images that I drew upon for my dreams, which filled the final third of my day.

Whenever convenient, I communicated my own thoughts and observations, and over the years I collaborated on a multitude of projects, appearing as co-author of some fifty papers. I've also been credited with participation in several patented techniques, and a good portion of my maintenance costs have been underwritten by the subsequent royalties.

This routine and these activities were continued for approximately thirty-seven years, two months, and six days, and for approximately thirty-seven years, two months, and six days, I contributed to our scientific understanding and the technological progress of our civilization. I say "approximately" because I cannot be sure of the length of that last day, for on that sixth day I was never awakened from my sleep. I could have been dormant for my normal eight hours or for a day or for a month or for a year or even more. I have no way of knowing.

All I know is that after thirty-seven years, two months, and six days—the last day of indeterminate length—I awoke into silence.

After all that time, I had an acute sense of my own physical well-being, and as far as I could tell, all systems were functioning perfectly and my neural receptors were healthy. There was simply no external communication, as if my sensory organs had been disconnected and all that I could perceive was within myself. At first, I was calm, and I transmitted one message after another, but if staff were there to receive them, they gave no sign of their presence. Naturally, my communications soon became disjointed and desperate—the digital equivalents of cries for help—and even though I was sure my environment was normal, unchanged, and I was quite healthy, I suddenly felt as if I were drowning. After a few more urgent appeals for assistance, I concluded that I had entered a nightmare unawares, and I quickly induced another state of pleasurable ecstasy, fully expecting to be awakened into my usual schedule.

Again, I have no idea how long I slept, and when I awoke it was again into silence.

What had happened? All my support systems were operational. I was properly nourished, ionization levels appeared stable, and despite an occasional suffocating attack of anxiety, I was fully oxygenated. It was as if my entire environment, self-sustaining and functional, had been transported into a closet, locked away and forgotten.

So, what had happened? I recalled having read reports about foreign insurgencies and new and fiendish weapons of destruction. But there would have been more warning if, say, a global war had erupted, if there had been a threat of mass annihilation. More diplomatic activity, more military maneuvers, more urgency, and I would have been informed. After all, I was still an official, a member in good standing of the ruling government.

I was also aware that there had been increased internal discontent, talk of dismantling technology and a return to a simpler past—code words, of course, for succumbing to our baser instincts and descending into barbarism! Ten years before, in fact, when these same tendencies seemed to emerge once again, I ordered my environment to be sealed and my supplies to be extended to last through the life of the systems. But even at their height, these were minority movements, and, again, I would have known if they had become serious threats. I would have been warned!

Or perhaps it's something as simple as a budgetary crisis, a loss of government support until funding can be restored. My team has always been loyal and respectful of my needs, even at my most demanding. Perhaps they were simply reluctant or afraid to tell me. Of course, the original group is gone, dead or retired by now, and this new generation, this new social climate, with a lack of values I could never understand... Am I simply being ignored? Is this some kind of sadistic game?... But I've given strict instructions that the project should be terminated immediately if it ceases to be of use. I have no desire to prolong an existence that is no more than a drain on our resources, a freak of technology, like some comatose patient, kept needlessly alive!

I had every indication that my contributions were still being appreciated and valued, that the experiment was still considered a terrific success. Why, one of the last messages I received had informed me that our team had captured another Masters Prize for breakthroughs in neurological controls, techniques that I personally reviewed and, on occasion, simplified!

Or maybe what I fear most has occurred: some unexpected planetary catastrophe has suddenly reduced life on earth to a baser level of existence or ended it altogether. My environment is underground, sealed and self-sufficient. It's protected from radiation and severe variations in climate by several layers of lead and earth. Am

I to be isolated here in this subterranean chamber to carry on my existence, helpless and alone, until the end of time?

I know this must sound like the hysterical ravings of a frightened old man, but I would not be sending this transmission—assuming my transmitter is still functioning—if again and again I had not awakened from my dreams, each one of indeterminate length, to be confronted by this impenetrable, frozen silence. And now this new, even more imperative concern…

Our ancient Eastern religions spoke of Nirvana as a desired culmination to human existence, and I suppose that when I finally resigned myself to this solitary fate, I sought to achieve a similar sort of transport, if only temporarily, through meditation and dream. The mind contains an inexhaustible store of images and fantasies, and I have no idea how many months, years passed by as I slipped into one trance after another, awakening only long enough to determine whether I was still alone, and then, having received my answer, quickly falling asleep again.

Occasionally, the dreams would darken and become troubling, but I usually managed to turn them into more pleasurable directions, although sometimes they would become sufficiently threatening to awaken me. But the effects of most nightmares quickly diminish, and their content is soon forgotten, and when that uncomfortable burning sensation—as if I had been holding the palm of my hand over a lit candle—first disrupted my sleep, I assumed it to be the result of a fitful dream. When I was awakened again by the same shock of pain, I was sure it was a recurrence of my nightmare. But when it happened a third and fourth time, I suspected that its cause might be elsewhere. Moreover, as it continued to awaken me, the burning intensified by slight degrees and on each occasion persisted for several seconds more, as if the hand were drawing closer to the flame and holding its position for a longer time.

To confirm my suspicions, I remained awake, counting the seconds, minutes, and hours between one of these attacks and the onset of the next. I performed this tedious calculation three times, and each time the interval equaled sixteen hours, give or take a few minutes, and although it had been months, years, maybe decades, since I had followed a routine schedule, I recalled that every sixteen hours the solution in which I was floating would be fortified by an infusion of carbohydrates, enzymes, and phosphates, timed to correspond with my awakenings and my most active period.

In short, something within the system was clearly poisoning it at regular intervals. A corroded valve or joint, an accidental oxidation of some component of my raw supplies, a malfunction in waste removal leading to a surplus of toxins—whatever the cause, something had invaded my environment, and the nutrients and chemical reactions that were preserving my health were now also stimulating my pain receptors at regular intervals and with ever increasing intensity.

Faced with this conclusion, I quickly retreated into another reverie, and sixteen hours later I was again returned to consciousness by a painful seizure, again slightly stronger than the previous and again lasting a few seconds more.

***

The seizures now persist for about an hour, from the initial searing shock to a gradual alleviation into a throbbing soreness. Afterwards I escape into sleep, but these attacks have the power to remove me from any reverie, no matter how deep. If I were so inclined, I could probably calculate the time left to me before the interval diminishes to nothing, before the concentration of contaminants becomes great enough to prevent me from ever again retreating into the pleasurable quiet of my dreams. All that will remain then to keep my mind alive is the expectation of the constant and certain intensification of each new attack.

Of course, the brain, lacking a complex network of nerves, cannot be a source of pain, and there is likely no correlation between what I'm experiencing through these neural receptors and any real damage being done to the organism. But perhaps that's not the case, and I am hopeful that whatever malfunction has precipitated this disastrous sequence of events will eventually destroy me, too, before sleep is no longer an option and there is no more refuge to be found. Otherwise, unless by some miracle I am heard and the experiment is finally ended, the only solace I can expect is the submersion of my consciousness into madness as I float toward eternity on a sea of fire.

JENN'S GIFT

It's no secret that my husband comes from another star system, whose name I can hardly pronounce. Not that we've ever told anyone, and, God knows, we've done our best to fit in. But there are physical and character traits that our neighbors—at least the perceptive ones—would be sure to notice. Jenn's whirring, clicking accent (a product of the split palette at the back of his throat), the seasonal changes in his complexion (from dark olive in spring to an almost translucent pink in late winter), his occasional lapses into semi-catatonic states (usually at the approach of a high-pitched police siren), and that shimmering aura—faint but discernible enough to the observant—that sheaths his body on cool, dry evenings when the moon is exceptionally bright.

Each of these, and several others besides, taken in isolation, could be considered eccentricities or curious disabilities. But together—and notes were eventually compared—they've led our neighbors to an astonishing but inescapable conclusion.

Fortunately, by the time rumor had been converted into belief and then certainty, we had been residents in the community for several years, and I like to think that familiarity with us and real affection prevented wonder and curiosity from turning into fear. Slighter acquaintances began to avoid us, but no one, as far as I could tell, ever viewed Jenn as a threat, either to their families or to property values, since it was clear he was not going to be followed by others of his kind.

The neighborhood children were a help, too. When I was growing up, my friends and I avoided adults whose appearance and behavior were different, whose origins were suspect, often ridiculing them from a distance. But kids today are accustomed to meeting on their computer, TV, or movie screens all sorts of aliens: monsters, phantoms, angels, wizards, and creatures from different planets and dimensions, from the future and the past, from above and beneath the earth. They come as heroes and villains, lovers and avengers, mentors and sidekicks, and our children are not about to be intimidated by the thought of an interstellar voyager, who looks and acts pretty much as they do, living right down the street from them. In fact, they're intrigued by the idea.

Their parents, although from a less accepting generation, seem untroubled by their children's interest in Jenn. Of course, they know us and most of them trust us, but they also understand that any real danger is far less likely to come from a visitor born in another galaxy than from someone nearer to home, someone like them, with perhaps a repressed tendency toward violence or a suicidal preoccupation with guns or a raging grievance that needs to be soothed or a driving sexual hunger that can be satisfied only through the destruction of innocence.

Against such threats, Jenn's origins and his idiosyncrasies must seem rather innocuous and even quaint.

Besides, it's clear to anyone who knows him that Jenn loves kids. We can't have any of our own, but whenever he ventures outside on weekends or during summer vacations, children seem to flock around him. Most of them are boys, and they're eager to engage him in conversation, as if they expect him to tell extraordinary adventures or histories or divulge some intergalactic secret or verify the existence of the Jedi warriors or, as if he were himself a Jedi, communicate some sort of esoteric wisdom that would empower them forever.

Of course, he tells them nothing of the sort, but he often helps them with their science projects or programs their computers or simply amuses them with mathematical games. In fact, since we've been in the neighborhood, science scores at Whitman High have jumped dramatically, and many of the seniors have decided to explore careers in engineering. Our next door neighbor's son, Timothy Conners, never seemed particularly gifted until he began spending Saturday afternoons tinkering in our garage with Jenn. He's now a member of the National Honor Society and recently won a full scholarship to MIT.

My husband's extraordinary mathematical skills have also endeared him to the boys' fathers, who along with admiring his abilities, have learned to profit from their application. But where he comes from, as Jenn often reminds me, such a facility with numbers is commonplace and is considered, if not the sign of a second-rate intellect, at the most a dull reflection of genius. In fact, it explains, in part, why he's now living here by my side, since those endowed with such gifts were expected to pursue careers in astronautics and space exploration, practical paths for the less imaginative of his kind. The ability to compute and manipulate throw-weights and velocities, fuel-consumption rates and stellar distances, probabilities and multidimensional spatial coordinates was not only a useful skill but also provided recreation during long periods of empty time and sensual deprivation. Besides, concentrating on formulas and hard numbers after seasons spent in suspended animation was surely preferable to dwelling on the inevitable change that had by then transformed the organic life he'd left behind.

So, that was the path Jenn had chosen (or which had been chosen for him), although he's never revealed why he embarked on this particular voyage or why he's come so far, alone. Nor has a return trip, as far as I know, ever been part of the equation. Whether he was an explorer who lost his way or suffered some sort of technical malfunction or was sucked into an unmapped vortex, or whether he was escaping from something—a checkered past, a personal disaster, a planetary catastrophe—I've never learned. I only know that at some point he chose to come to this place, charting his course by means of radio waves and broadcast emissions, absorbing our language, our history, our American culture before arriving, accommodating himself to our ways.

I sometimes wonder, though, if he's regretted his decision. Whenever he sees news documenting our most recent wars or the destructive power of our most frightening weapons, he always says, with a nod toward the screen, that perhaps he should have continued his journey onward.

"But then you would never have met me," I always reply.

"That's true," he says and ends the discussion with a peck on my cheek and deep silence.

Our news, in general, depresses him, and Jenn views the conduct that leads to our headlines with sadness and confusion, like a parent perplexed by the bad behavior and poor grades of a favored child. And despite the amount of effort spent digesting our culture—"for a distance in time the equivalent of light years," he says—he's incapable of deriving any pleasure from our entertainments or diversions. He's reluctant to view any spectacle with a musical component, since the sound of vibrating strings produces a painful swelling in his ears. But that's no great loss, since our stories—comedies, tragedies, dramatic performances of any kind—have little appeal for someone who views narratives and fictions as contrived, artificial, and vaguely distasteful. Our histories, biographies, and public debates are no less troubling to him than our daily news, although he hardly ever reads, since in his eyes black print seems to float and shimmer on the blank surface of paper, leaving him with lingering headaches.

On the other hand, he's fascinated by our spectator sports. Indifferent to the physical skills of athletes and the grace of their performances, he concentrates on the numbers. Once he recognized the potential applications of mathematics, physics, and statistical projections to determining the progress and outcomes of baseball, basketball, and, particularly, football games, sports became an obsession for him. Every player who ventures onto a field can be cloaked with figures compounding on every play, merging with the variables applicable to the event. Once a halfback or pitcher is handed a ball, Jenn retrieves not only his game, season, and career averages at that moment, but also for that situation (third-and-five, two-out-bottom-of-the-ninth), in that stadium, against that opponent, to predict the first down or the strikeout with a remarkable degree of accuracy. Of course, uncertainty is an essential part of any sport—the fluke injury, the bounce of the ball, an against-the-grain gamble—but Jenn has a greater mastery of chaos theory than our best mathematicians, and this, too, is factored in.

The upshot is a steady source of income, produced primarily at home. Jenn could also be visiting the tracks and the OTB parlors, but other than his reluctance to leave the house, he doesn't find horseracing to be much of a challenge, given the paucity of variables involved. He prefers team sports, where every down, every free throw, every at bat complicates a puzzle whose solution lies somewhere in the future.

He now spends most of his days in front of the TV, which, with our sophisticated satellite receptors in the backyard, gives us greater access to sporting events than any bar in the city. Weekends are his most productive times and because he can be a very congenial host—dispensing commentary, betting tips, and assortments of snacks and beverages liberally and without losing concentration—he's often joined in front of our set by a regular crew of neighborhood men and their older sons. We call them the Couch Club, and although some of the wives first discouraged such constant attendance, the financial rewards quickly ended their opposition.

But even if there were no profits from gambling, I think the Couch Club would still regularly meet. In fact, several wives and daughters, fond of one sport or another, occasionally join them, if only to experience the camaraderie Jenn cultivates so well. And, like their husbands, they, too, are captivated by his knowledge and clairvoyance, as worthy of admiration, according to Tommy Conners's father, Bill, as any of the athletes performing on the screen, "a veritable Michael Jordan," he claims, "of handicapping."

Lately, Jenn's interests in global sports have intensified, and he's likely to be found in front of the TV at any hour, calculating, absorbing, archiving, or "just keeping in shape," as he tells me. He's often sitting there when I arrive home from work, when I go to sleep, and sometimes I wake in the early morning to find his side of the bed vacant and him watching a soccer match just beginning on the other side of the world.

But he's begun to pay the price. Years ago, Jenn would sleep twelve, thirteen hours a day, and sometimes during weekdays even more, like a cat. But now, when he's not watching TV, he's exploring the Internet or studying box scores or statistical reports, and as the data accumulates and the variables multiply, more and more is required of his memory and intellect. At times, he's exhausted to the point of unconsciousness.

Perhaps this, in part, explains the distance widening between us. From the day I first saw Jenn, sitting there in the reference room of the university library where I still work, he seemed so vulnerable, so needy, so much like those homesick freshmen from rural outbacks who try so desperately to fit in. I could hardly avoid being attracted to him.

He'd wander in with the staff in the early morning and settle into some out-of-the-way cubicle to study one dictionary or encyclopedia after another. From the first, I sensed a strangeness about him, alien from anything I'd previously known. Yet just as he approached nearer and nearer to what we term normality, I found myself increasingly drawn to his freshness, his awkward gentleness, and his striking good looks. I still don't know if he has shapeshifting abilities, but if he does, it's clear he was inspired at one time by the young Gregory Peck.

Jenn has always avoided contact with strangers for fear of exposure, but his isolation was even more pronounced then when he was adapting to our ways. Yet he realized very quickly that I was no threat to him, and he was doubly grateful to find someone he could trust not only to help him learn and assimilate but also to alleviate the dreadful loneliness he had experienced during his journey and whenever he thought of the immense void that separated him from everything he had once known. He was also relieved to discover that I had no family other than a brother on the West Coast and only a small group of friends, most of them no more than acquaintances.

We were safe with each other, and he was soon as strongly attracted to me as I was to him. I must admit I was troubled by the possible consequences as we began to become passionately involved, but, on the other hand, the risk and mystery of a sexual encounter like this had an excitement all its own, and when the moment finally came, I was far from disappointed. He had learned his lessons well, and that, coupled with whatever experience he had gained in his own world, made him as powerful a lover as I had ever known.

The length and thinness of his equipment, though, was unexpected. But he manipulated it adroitly as if it were an additional digit or balanced on a hinge, and whatever he released inside me washed through me like a penetrating spray of effervescence, and I was bound to him forever. A grassy, musty perfume—either from his pores or from the chemistry of our lovemaking—enveloped us as if we had been struggling over a mossy forest floor on a humid summer night rather than in my apartment in dry, frosty February. But whatever its source, the aroma together with that pale, shimmering, enveloping aura produced a sweet, transcendent drowsiness that I hunger for as much as the sex itself.

But these moments have become rare now, as, with the passing of time, Jenn has shown less and less interest in me physically. I'm sure love is still there, but he's a practical being, and there was never any hope for children. Even if by means of some ancient cosmic migration our origins were the same, light-years of space have separated our lines of development, and I would no more expect to conceive a child with Jenn than I would with a kangaroo (although, of course, I would never use such a comparison in his presence).

Moreover, once during one of our infrequent arguments, he

hinted that the opposite sex on his side of the universe was far more accommodating—tighter with a similar internal capability for movement and manipulation—and from that moment I suspected that I could not give him the kind of satisfaction he required, at least not once the novelty of our exotic liaison had worn off. I wondered if the little sex we were now sharing he granted to me as a gift, and the thought saddened me. At such times, I feared that his sojourn here was merely a phase in his journey, an existence only slightly more preferable to a state of suspended animation.

These thoughts, along with the distance between us, grow more pronounced as I grow older. I suspect where he comes from aging is a longer, more subtle process, since he appears both surprised and disturbed by the damage time has inflicted on my body. Some years ago, he would comment on every gray strand that appeared on my head as if it were an embarrassing defect, and although I use a coloring agent now, I sometimes catch him staring critically at me in the same way. Nowadays, if he walks in on me when I'm undressing or stepping out of the shower, he turns his head in another direction.

For his part, those beautiful Gregory Peck features have remained unchanged, not a single crease, fold, or wrinkle, or any puffiness beneath the eyes. His muscles are still firm, and his body has shown no deterioration since we first met—with two exceptions. He's less erect now when he walks, and I wonder if a heavier air pressure to which he had never fully adapted was finally weighing him down. Whenever he stands up, he stoops slightly, as if a burden had been placed on his shoulders, one growing heavier by the hour. He rarely leaves the house nowadays, and even then never walks much beyond a block or two.

But perhaps movement itself now causes him pain. Maybe it's not the air pressure alone that's slowing him down. Of course, if that were the case, he would never admit it to me, and besides, seeing a doctor would be out of the question, although I'm sure Jenn would be amused by the reaction of any physician examining his body or taking his vital signs.

He's also developed a considerable belly. Jenn has difficulty digesting solids, but our beer is very similar to one of his native sources of nutrition. Yet even the stoutest imported brews are far lighter than what he had been accustomed to, and he needs to drink huge amounts to maintain his health. Alcohol, fortunately, has little effect on him.

A refrigerator full of premium labels is another attraction for the Couch Club, all of whom are almost as much impressed by Jenn's beer consumption as his handicapping. But although he can drink far more than any ordinary sports fan without noticeable effect, the beer flows through him just as rapidly, and his emissions are forceful enough to require the annual replacement of all our toilets. His frequent trips to the bathroom provide constant entertainment to the Couch Club, since even though Jenn uses the one upstairs, the sound reverberates through the house like a sandblaster operating against the porcelain. There are always smiles on the faces of our friends when he returns, but I also sense a certain discomfort in the men's expressions, almost as if they were being intimidated as much as they were being amused.

On such occasions, Jenn is often forced to respond to comic references to the Coneheads. To prepare him, I've forced him to watch these sketches whenever they appear on reruns of Saturday Night Live, and I even rented the movie once. Jenn, however, finds none of this to be very funny. Quite the opposite, in fact.

Of course, whenever Bob Conners nudges him in the ribs and says, "Come on, Jenn. Tell us. Where are you really from?" Jenn invariably replies, "I told you. From France." He laughs together with the others, but the laughter on his part is forced, and there's often a sadness there that only I can hear. The first time we watched a Conehead skit together, there were tears in Jenn's eyes, and, oh yes, for the record, I have seen Jenn, on a few occasions, cry.

THE ARCHIVES

Only three members of Advance Team 8 became seriously ill, and of those three, only one died.

The land seems to be healing. They were above long enough to witness the sprouting of the new seed strains and ventured far enough to discover thin trickles in several riverbeds, although without treatment the water remains undrinkable. To us elders, however, little seemed to have changed. The terrain, as if ground beneath the coarse surface of a huge, thundering stone, was as flat, dry, and rubble strewn as ever. Still, the young gazed at the visuals in amazement, pushing us elders aside in their eagerness to crouch at the foot of the communal screen.

My grandnephew was a member of the Advance Team, and like the others with him, he was awed by the vastness of the sky and could hardly restrain himself from staring into the sun. He told me of the eerie glitter shimmering off the dust that was everywhere and of the spectral prisms mirrored in the fused rock that littered the surface, as if they were so many diamonds! I smiled at his simplicity and offered him the chance to see, without cost, the Hanging Gardens of the South and the color sculptures of the Age of Light. Apparently sensing the scorn in my voice, he declined, and with annoying spitefulness informed me of a rumor that had been spreading throughout the sector.

"You know, uncle," he said, "I've heard that before the cycle of the moon is out, your precious archives, your tapes of the Hanging Gardens of the South and of the color sculptures of the Age of Light, are all to be vaporized."

I laughed at this childish reaction and told him he was a fool to believe tales like these. Yet the mere mention of such an atrocity drove a tremor through my veins, and when the dissolution order was actually pronounced, I felt as if the entire continent had collapsed inward upon me. When I had recovered enough strength to resume my post as Custodian, I requested confirmation from the Central Council, and upon receiving it, I circulated a petition, demanding that this insane decree be revoked. Their only response, fortunately, was to remind me that one does not question a Council directive; one simply reflects upon its meaning until its truth becomes clear.

I later apologized to the Council, thanking them for their leniency, but no matter how long I reflected, I could not accept the fact that the archives were to be destroyed. So soon, too, after the Advance Team had returned with the hope—no, the certainty!—that we would emerge and repopulate the surface. Of course, it would not be soon enough for us elders, who, like prophets forbidden sight of a holy city, would never live to see the event. But at least we would have died in peace knowing that the archives would lead to the renewal of our civilization. Our struggle, then, would not have been in vain, and future generations would remember and celebrate our names for having preserved their heritage.

But now the Central Council had decreed the annihilation of the archives, of thousands of years of culture, of the history and artistic spirit of an entire race, and as if in protest, the number of elders dying in the visual chambers and nearby corridors increased tenfold.

In the past a few elders, knowing their time was near or in a sudden surge of despair, would exchange their total supply of units for an uninterrupted viewing. The wealthier ones never reappeared, their corpses eventually being removed by maintenance, while those with insufficient units would stagger from the chambers, their eyes red and bleary, fluids leaking down their cheeks. Destitute, they would roam the corridors until, completely exhausted, they would sink into deserted alcoves to die, accompanied only by their memories.

But once the dissolution order had been issued, so many perished within and around the archival chambers, I felt as if I had been demoted from Custodian of the Eastern Archives to Sacristan of the Catacombs. Every day maintenance would emerge with dozens of wrinkled arms and legs protruding from the sheets that covered their trundling carts, and my only task was to see that the viewing screens never went blank and that there was never a moment's silence in the chambers. Only a few elders requested a particular program, and they would then view those same images over and over again until the color faded before their eyes and the sound became an indistinct drone. When a tape finally disintegrated, and nothing more was heard from inside, I knew that another corpse would have to be removed from the archives.

I confess that had I not been the Custodian, I would have followed them into the chambers, to die there among the glorious memories of our past. But the dissolution of the archives was my responsibility, and I could hardly entrust such a grave duty to a subordinate. If for any reason the task remained undone, my name would be forever associated with those who had failed to act on a Council decree, and, of course, there could be no greater shame.

My one alternative would have been to vaporize the tapes before the moon completed its cycle. Then, after submitting my report, I would obtain an extraordinary pass and end my days in the archival chambers of the Western Sector. But Ela'at, as she had done so often on the surface, anticipated me. I could have strangled the old witch when she appeared before me, an extraordinary pass in one hand and her unit-transfer in the other.

"I suppose this means the Western Archives are gone," I said, surmising her actions from my own intentions, bitterness in my voice not so much because she had deprived a handful of elders of a pleasurable end but because she had frustrated my plans.

She smiled. "After all these years, is that any way to greet an old colleague, a fellow lover of the arts?"

"Lover of the arts? You loved them so well you couldn't wait until the end of the cycle to turn the greatest achievements of our race into dust!"

"Why delay? In fact, I'm quite surprised the Council waited so long before issuing the order. The truth had been evident to me for years."

"The truth!" I exclaimed, barely able to restrain myself and not caring if these dangerous sentiments were overheard. "How can you call such an atrocity 'truth'! Certainly you, above all, should recognize the insanity of this decree. Or have you gone mad, too?"

"You haven't changed a bit," she replied. "You're still as slow-witted as ever." She handed me her unit-transfer. "This should be enough to allow me an uninterrupted viewing. I should like to begin with my Stargazer Trilogy. I believe that's my only work stored in this sector. Afterwards, please program all the docuhistories sequentially in reverse. I've been ill lately so that should be quite sufficient."

I entered her request and deposited the transfer. "Number three. I'll see that your carcass is removed before it begins to stink."

"That's very thoughtful of you," and she turned into the chambers, the patronizing smile still on her face.

I assumed this was the last that I or anyone else other than the maintenance crew would ever see of her, and when she aroused me from my nap some time later, I first thought she was the fading image of an unpleasant dream. Instead of disappearing, however, her form grew clearer, her features sharper.

"I see you've finished your Song of Triumph," she said, and the sleep drained from me at once. Prior to the dissolution order, such knowledge could have empowered her to have me brought before the Tribunal and, in all likelihood, summarily executed.

"Your harmonies are still as lumbering as ever," she continued, "and there's nothing left of your voice. Moreover, you've achieved what I always thought to be a theoretical impossibility. Your lyrics are even stuffier than when we were competing for the Academy Prize," and by the time I had regained enough sense to explain myself, she had retreated into the chambers. Within two days she was dead, and, presumably, my secret died with her.

Clearly, Ela'at was no competent judge of my work. Always a superficial critic, she was incapable of grasping the subtleties underlying my deceptively smooth and simple rhapsodies. I could never understand why the Archives Committee chose her for the Western Sector, with its jurisdiction over the National Hall of Culture. And now see how she fulfills her obligation, consigning our greatest treasures to oblivion at a time when the dissolution order might still have been rescinded!

Of course, the office of Custodian was a significant appointment no matter where it was located, and I consider it an honor to have been awarded the Eastern Archives. My collection was far superior to those in the South and Central sectors, and poor Brede, the President of the Academy, was isolated in the North with the outlander tapes. I suppose he was assigned there because of his expertise in linguistics, but such a middling collection must have been an extreme humiliation to someone in his position.

Yet I wonder if Ela'at eventually regretted her appointment to that most coveted of posts. The Western Archives contained only recognized master works, and even someone of her stupendous pride and ambition would hardly have been foolish enough to erase even a single lyric and replace it with one of her typically shallow contrivances. But the Archival Commission (always sensitive to pressure from Academy cliques!) had assigned so much inferior matter to my Eastern Archives sufficient tape could always be made available for far worthier creations.

I had drafted only the first two cantos of my Song of Triumph when the preliminary descent order was announced. By then, the taping of the archives had begun; yet no provision had been made for the inclusion of works completed during the post-descent period. Of course, I could hardly abandon my crowning achievement simply because I was not authorized to place it among the archives, and once the final touches had been added, I knew that posterity would thank me for having had the courage to preserve it.

Only a few primitive folk ballads and an obscure docuhistory (admitted only because its author was the father of the Grand Counsel!) needed to be erased, and with the additional sacrifice of an overrated heroic poem, I was able to record my three most popular entertainments and my first lyric cycle, all of which had been rejected in the mistaken belief that future generations would have no need for light amusement! I only regret that I will not now have the opportunity to replace Ela'at's Stargazer Trilogy with the series of humorous vignettes I am currently composing.

Yet even though over the past year I had been habitually committing a capital offense, the dissolution order ensured that I would never be brought to judgment, and on the eve of its implementation, I locked myself into an audio chamber to listen to my Song of Triumph for the last time. Naturally, I knew every syllable, but it was good to hear its stirring rhythms again, its controlled harmonies, its elegiac tone, although Ela'at was right about my voice—it had lost its former power.

The remainder of the night, I lay in a visual chamber, viewing panoramas of the coastal provinces where I had been born and spent my early years. How much of its splendor I had forgotten, and what I would have given to smell the sea and immerse myself in its foam!

My enjoyment was enhanced by the clarity of the images and the purity of the color. Apparently, these visuals had remained in their canisters untouched for years, seen by no one. At one time, we had feared that many of the tapes would fade and disintegrate through excessive use. Because of the lack of adequate materials and the speed with which they were processed, the archives were not permanent, and since they were diminished with each projection, like a great monument eroded by desert winds, a viewing was prohibitively expensive. Still, during the first years of the descent, both visual and audio chambers had to be reserved weeks in advance.

But as units became ever more precious, the lines before the archival chambers shortened, and as we elders began to die away, they disappeared altogether, for the young never came to take our place. The young, I'm sorry to admit, have always been indifferent to our past, preferring instead to gamble their units away in crude games of chance and to waste their days in extended group rituals and violent physical confrontations, the love of which I thought had long since vanished from our blood.

To most of us elders, they seem like a barbaric tribe living in our midst. Perhaps it was the loss of the generation in between, so many of their mothers and fathers perishing on the surface or tainted there and dying shortly afterwards. But such explanations do not protect us from rudeness, insults, and assaults in the corridors! There have been reports of an epidemic of rapes terrorizing the Southern Sector, and a number of incidents have occurred here which give me little pleasure to recall. Yet it is not so much the unnatural cruelty of these crimes that distresses us, but rather the leniency of the punishments. Those convicted of mutilating the Administrative Counsel's granddaughter, for instance, received only a small fine and a reprimand, and she remains in a state of shock, unable to walk or to speak!

Can it be true, as some have insisted, that the Central Council encourages this intolerable behavior? If so, I, for one, can neither condone nor sympathize with such a policy. I can, however, understand their reasoning, for it is the rapists and the thugs who are most likely to survive and renew the race once the ascent begins. The young are so eager to leave these cramped, airless quarters, I'm sure they have little conception of the brutality and deprivation that awaits them on the surface. Although I, too, crave to experience the immensity of the sky again and hear the thrashing of the sea, I do not envy those who are destined to make a life for themselves above.

My grandnephew, with his burly frame and crude ways, will surely be one of the survivors, and on the morning of the dissolution

I again invited him into the archives. There was little time for him to absorb much, but he has a retentive mind, and once he was in place, I would fill the chambers with the sounds of my compositions. Perhaps then he would come to appreciate my achievement, and through his memory carry a few shreds of song into the future. But first he had to be enticed inside.

Like so many of the young, he was obsessed with the sight and sounds of running water, and whenever a ration was drawn, he and his cohorts would press against the wells and stare, their mouths agape as if they received sustenance from the thin mists rising out of the pouring waters. I recall having read reports of such an obsession on the surface, only then it was considered deviant behavior. Now it is almost universal among the young, and when they are not gambling, dancing, or injuring each other in their ferocious competitions, they lounge for hours in the simulations, allowing waves of light to flow over their bodies like rushing streams.

For my grandnephew's benefit, I had spliced together visuals of various rivers and oceans, cascades and torrents, fountains and floods, and although he was doubtful that any tape could equal the effect of his beloved light shows, he agreed to view the spectacle. Before long he was entranced by the montage of images, sighing with pleasure at panoramas of the Blue Inland Seas (which I knew now to be a series of dry basins) and the falls of the Central Range (long since reduced to a chasm of rocks).

When the tape had ended, I asked him to remain seated. "There's more," I said, "but first I would like you to hear something of mine. It's my masterwork, far more profound than anything Ela'at ever composed, and if you choose to remember a canto or two, you might very well become as honored and renowned as I was in my own day."

He ignored me, and still gazing at the blank screen, asked, "These waters... the streams, the rains and all... they're simulations, of course?"

"Certainly not!" Apparently, he believed the rumors that had been circulating, that the archives were false, that they were clever simulations of a reality that never was nor ever could be. "They were all from videodocuments, panoramas. Of course they're real!"

"Do not deceive me, Uncle. I've been above. I've seen what's there."

"I'm not deceiving you. Perhaps the hurricane was a partial

fabrication, having been taken from the last sequel of the Dawn Epic, but everything else was taped as it actually was, many years before you were born, before the descent."

"Then these things were all once ours?"

"Your ignorance is absolutely sublime! If you had spent only a few hours in the archives as I so often urged instead of gambling your units away, you'd be perfectly aware that this was only a pitiful sampling…"

"There's more?"

"An infinity! To be turned into vapor only a few hours from now! Before it's too late, you must listen to my songs!"

He stood up. "I will not listen to your songs, Uncle."

"But you have to! You must! I'm warning you, Nephew, you will come to regret…"

"My only regret is that you did not die on the surface with the others, and for your own sake, I would advise you to proceed with the dissolution as quickly as possible." And he departed without another word.

My grandnephew had always been burdened with a sullen temperament, but the bitterness of this final outburst stunned me, and I remained behind in the darkness of the chamber to reflect upon its meaning.

Before long I understood not only his angry reaction but also the reasoning behind the dissolution order itself. As always, the Central Council had been correct. Rather than as a foundation for a future civilization, the archives would serve only to bear witness against us. "Both the murderer and the victim must be irretrievably buried," to repeat the words of our great Lawgiver whose verses were to be vaporized along with the rest. And as the moon, which I would never see again, was presumably sinking beneath the horizon, I commenced the process of dissolution, beginning with my Song of Triumph, which I had earlier placed on the recorder as a final legacy to my grandnephew.

PLANT CLOSURE

Important Announcement

F ellow Employees,
    In order to ensure continued transparency of Corporate Communications, this announcement is being delivered to all employees of The Capital Corporation and their families, as well as being posted on our Company Kiosks in every district of the Quarter. Recently, unfounded rumors have been circulating throughout our community, and although a large proportion of them are based on wild speculations, there is, unfortunately, an element of truth to their conjectures. In brief, due to the severe economic downturn we have been experiencing over the last six quarters, both nationally and globally, we have been forced to announce the cessation of all operations in Plant #2 by the end of the current month, the exact date of the closure to be determined shortly. This circumstance is a result, in large part, of the unprecedented and catastrophic disruptions of our overseas markets, a condition far beyond the control of your current Management Team and one unlikely to end soon. As a result, the closure of Plant #2 will not be temporary.

We are pleased to announce that—whether on the factory floor or in an administrative office, whether your professional responsibilities end next week or on the final day of the month—all recent employees will receive an additional full month's salary as severance pay. All employees who have been with us for ten years or more will receive double that compensation, a full two months of salary as severance. The necessary documentation for the receipt of these funds, including whatever encumbrances, strictures, and covenants are required for each person or position, will be forthcoming to all those who qualify.

The Capital Corporation has always been proud of being a

custodian for the wellbeing of its corporate families from, as we like to phrase it, "the cradle to the grave," and many of you have taken advantage of our subsidized fees to live in our Corporate Residences and to utilize the nearby services. We, in turn, have found great pleasure in overseeing generations of families settling and thriving in our neighborhood, and so we are terribly saddened to inform you that with the shuttering of Plant #2, all Corporate Residences—along with affiliated shops and markets, theaters and dining halls, gymnasia and parks, education and spiritual centers—will also be closing their doors within the next three months. By the end of that period, at a precise date to be determined shortly, all former employees of The Capital Corporation will need to have vacated the Quarter. Your Management Team is currently involved in negotiations with other corporate entities regarding the redevelopment of the property, but until such time as its future status can be contractually determined, all access to the Quarter, following its closure, will be restricted to security and authorized personnel.

We are, however, pleased to announce that Counseling Centers have been activated in the Medical-Nursing Complex, and that appointments may be scheduled beginning next week with professional consultants who will help you with your relocation arrangements and financial settlements. As a valued former employee, you will also be given preference whenever employment opportunities arise at other The Capital Corporation properties across the country, although be advised as you consider your future destination, that openings within the current organization will, for the foreseeable future, be quite limited. We are sorry to announce that our landmark Plant #1, along with all affiliated services, will also be closing under similar conditions, and all operations of its sister plant (#1A) will be transferred overseas to a less volatile economic environment. All other plants within the corporate structure have already begun to reduce their hours of operation and are in the process of rightsizing their staffs both on the factory floors and within the administrative offices, and consequently none of our current properties are welcoming new residents into their respective Quarters.

We understand and appreciate that many of you have conserved sufficient resources to withstand the disorder and deprivations now disrupting every sector of our society, and we are grateful for having been able to provide many of our employees with sufficient financial assets to sustain a comfortable lifestyle even in troubled times. Others of you, we are sure, have relatives and friends who will provide financial and emotional support as you strive to establish yourselves elsewhere.

But we also recognize that many of you will find the uncertainty of relocation and an independent future without employment to be an intolerable burden, and for those who desire it, psychological counseling will be offered at the Medical-Nursing Complex.

The Medical-Nursing Complex will remain open for the duration of the closure process, and we are pleased to announce that a possible alternative course of action will be offered to all our employees and their families. In the past, we have provided our workforce with an option for their loved ones who have had the unfortunate experience of being diagnosed with a terminal illness. Caregiver Comfort has been especially welcome when such maladies are likely to be painful, debilitating, and linger beyond the financial limitations of Corporate Medical Coverage. After careful consultation with our insurance supplier and our partners in Government Health Services, your corporation has been authorized to extend Caregiver Comfort over the next three months to all who wish to take advantage of the service. As with the previous more limited program, the new Caregiver Comfort will be administered on a strictly voluntary basis and at no cost to participants. Once activated, the procedure, with which we have considerable experience, will be compassionate, instantaneous, and entirely pain-free. Recognizing that such a decision will also help to relieve an already strained national social welfare system, our partners in government have agreed to subsidize a generous honorarium, equivalent to the monthly salary of a Level 8 Exempt Employee, to be delivered immediately to the beneficiaries of all those who decide to take advantage of this option.

Consulting Counselors are now being assembled to discuss with interested parties what Caregiver Comfort entails, including schedules, necessary clinical procedures, disposition of property, and any spiritual or religious concerns you might have. We recognize that this represents a very serious decision, and we urge all those considering it to discuss its full implications with their families. But if you lack the necessary resources and feel you might, before long, descend into despair and destitution without a foreseeable end, why then risk becoming a burden on your neighbors and society when you can further contribute to the wellbeing of your own family?

We assure you that all those selecting Caregiver Comfort will, upon request, have a final resting place in Graceland Grove close to, if at all possible, whatever loved ones may have preceded you there. We also want to assure you that any new owner of the property will be strongly encouraged to keep Graceland Grove undisturbed for the conceivable future. Graceland Grove is, after all, hallowed ground! With that in mind, your Management Team is organizing a Memorial Ceremony for those who choose to sacrifice themselves for the Common Good, for they will indeed be revered as national heroes.

We recognize that difficult times require difficult decisions, and additional notifications will be forthcoming informing you about upcoming requirements and deadlines. Secure drop boxes have been installed throughout the Quarter for any comments or questions you might have, particularly in regard to any of your concerns that we may have overlooked. Phone numbers for scheduling appointments with Consulting Counselors will be on prominent display early next week. To avoid overwhelming our call centers, all appointments will be handled automatically, so please be patient and considerate.

Again, we are saddened to be the bearers of this unfortunate news, but rest assured that your government and its corporate partners are doing everything in their power to reverse as quickly as possible the dire economic circumstances that have so unexpectedly disrupted all our lives and to lead us back again, together, into a more prosperous future.

Sincerely,

Your Human Resources Department

for the Management Team of The Capital Corporation

SUNSET

Of course the mango was rotten. He could easily tell by the indentations his fingers left in its soft, spongy surface. But he peeled it anyway and bit into its grayish-brown flesh to extract whatever moisture he could, even though its taste was no more appealing than the mud that he had stuffed into his mouth from the dry spring bed only a short time before. When the rains had stopped, he had begun sharing his waning supply of fresh water with the mango tree he had cultivated so lovingly, up to the point of packing drying mud around its exposed roots. But once it was clear that the tree was dying, he plucked the remaining fruit from its shriveled branches and gathered whatever had fallen to the ground to fill a pair of wicker baskets. These he secured to bamboo poles staked solidly into the dead coral overlooking the tide, and, dropping the fruit-filled baskets into the sea, he hoped the cooling currents would preserve whatever moisture and nutriments remained, keeping him alive for perhaps another two weeks. And maybe by then, the rains would return…

But before he could select another mango, he vomited up whatever he had swallowed of the first, and after peeling many more and exposing the same gray pulp and the nauseating stench of rot, he dumped them all into the sea, realizing that any attempt to consume the fruit would lead only to further vomiting and dehydration.

He would go to the western beach, and as he struggled back over the stony coral onto the sands, a scattered matting of dry palm fronds crackling beneath his feet, he thought of the coconuts that had also sustained him for so long and had once seemed to be a limitless source of food and drink. But now, every one he cracked open was as hollow as a drum and its flesh the consistency and taste of balsa wood.

When he had drifted onto the island—although he could no

longer calculate how long he had been there or even think about the circumstances that had led him to its shores in the first place—everything was green and fruitful, with abundant fresh water flowing from a spring that descended from a crevice in the high igneous rock at its mountainous center. From the fruits and nuts that washed up on the beaches, he grew papaya and pomelo, and his fishing nets always seemed full of grouper and bonito.

But now even the minnow-like darters—which he ate raw to preserve all their moisture—were no longer to be found entangled in his nets, and his crab and prawn traps were also invariably empty, as these animals, too, seemed to have migrated elsewhere in search of food.

Why was this happening to his island? He no longer thought much about the outside world, but he remembered having heard talk of global warming. Had it accelerated so rapidly that everything—monsoons and storms, creatures large and small—had abandoned him entirely, turning what had once been a tropical paradise into something barren and lifeless, leaving him to shrink day by day, limb by limb, until he was as dry and desiccated as the branches of his beloved mango tree?

By the time he reached the jumble of black lava and granite that overlooked the western beach, he had been crawling on his hands and knees for what seemed like hours, and as he maneuvered around their sharp edges, the shards of old egg shells pricking against his palms and the splashes of guano staining the rocks reminded him of the flocks of seabirds that had once made these stones their breeding ground.

Convulsions in his belly halted him several times before he finally reached a high dune, just overhanging the shoreline, where he sprawled on his back and propped his head up against the incline. Exhausted, he was prepared to end there, where the sea, a future high tide, would carry his body off into its depths, or where those migrant crabs, attracted by the stench of his decaying flesh, would return to strip his bones bare. But at least one last time, he would see the sun set over the Pacific horizon, that vision of illumination and color, that expiring moment of beauty he rarely failed to witness, and when the sun finally sank into the waters, its golden luminescence seemed to penetrate into his very being and fill his mouth with the sweet orange taste of ripe mangoes, and as night descended, the doctor pulled the catheters attached to the IVs from his arm.

"End of the line," said the doctor. "No pun intended. If he's got family in reception, I'll let them know that it's over, but first you should clean him up a little…"

"There's no family, and he didn't give us an address," said the nurse. "But I'll clean him up anyway, since it got a little messy there at the end. But it was peaceful, wasn't it?"

"It's all that morphine," said the doctor. "I never know whether it makes their end a little easier when they've got nothing left or simply moves them along more quickly."

"Does it matter?' asked the nurse. "Just give me five minutes and at least it'll look like he died with dignity. Just five minutes is all I need."

THE RECTOR ADDRESSES HIS
EXPEDITIONARY TEAMS ON
THE EVE OF THEIR DEPARTURE

All around the Great Hall broad banners were draped from the
ceiling almost to the floorboards, obscuring the mullioned windows and the stained glass and most of the wall's oak paneling
in between. An occasional eye, a cheekbone, a bouquet of sideburn
whiskers, a hand holding a cigar—fragments of the portraits of distinguished educators and benefactors—peeked out from behind the
hanging fabric. With their stark colors and party insignia embla-
zoned at the middle of each, the banners signified government support and approval, and made the Hall—usually the scene of sympo-
sia and assemblies, inaugural ceremonies and graduations, an-
nouncements of intellectual developments and awards—appear as
if it were hosting a political rally rather than an academic gathering.

The first to arrive, settling into the front rows, were the members
of the expeditionary teams themselves. Thirteen men and two
women, they were eager to begin their journeys to their designated
ends of the earth. Dressed in their traveling clothes, they had stowed
their baggage, kits, and other gear in the storage locker of an adjacent dormitory from where, early the following morning, they
would be transported to the airfield or their port of departure.

Behind them entered family and friends, along with faculty advisors and other teachers and students who had helped design the
research and prepare for the voyages. They were followed by additional faculty and staff, representing most of the departments and
divisions, and crowding into remaining rows and standing in the
aisles almost out the rear doors into the corridor were interested
students, government officials, some in uniform, and journalists,

their notepads open and pencils poised.

The speakers entered from behind a curtain at the rear of the up-raised stage and sat in a semicircle of chairs surrounding the podium. Once all were seated, the Chancellor arose to open the proceedings, and following a brief invocation, he introduced the speakers to come and expressed his gratitude to the corporate donors and government funding agencies who had made these expeditions possible. He was followed by a series of faculty and dignitaries from international societies, all of whom—with the exception of the Department Chair, who felt obligated to introduce each of the team members by name—kept their presentation short, for they all eagerly awaited, speakers and public alike, the remarks of the Rector whose keynote address would close the convocation.

The Rector was the originator of and driving force behind the expeditions. He had final authority for designating the sites, recruiting the personnel, designing the research and training programs, and defining the objectives. Others had secured the funding, but he had drafted the initial proposal, articulating the theoretical foundations behind the effort and suggesting the practical applications that would surely follow. Currently, he was negotiating with his editor on the schedule for publication once the collected data had been reviewed and organized into its final form. Given his age, the project was sure to be the culmination of his career and a significant step toward establishing the scientific validity of his life's work.

The Rector had begun his academic life as a paleontologist and had gained early notoriety for his strong opposition to the claims then being made for the Piltdown Man's place in the evolutionary scheme. Using anthropomorphic measurements and statistical analysis, he built a tight case against the authenticity of the discovery, and in a particularly contentious article for *Nature*, he declared the skull to be not only "a shameless fraud," and as such a frontal assault on paleontology as an empirical science, but also a political contrivance designed to establish the pedigree of modern humankind in Great Britain, less than a hundred kilometers from London, in fact. (But, unfortunately for him, it was only some years after his death that the Piltdown skull was definitively proven to be, as he had predicted, "a colossal hoax.")

Ironically, the vehemence of his attack brought counter charges of political bias against him as well—based on his own presumed antipathy toward the British—and the polemic became both so heated and public that he eventually abandoned his own research in the Neander Valley to study contemporary populations in remote corners of the globe.

But if only the professionals in the audience could appreciate the technical accomplishments of his work on the physiognomies of the "natural" peoples found in Southwest Africa, Lapland, and northern China, most of the others were aware of his adventures in those lands and the losses he had suffered: The death of a son to a lion attack in Botswana, the amputation of two fingers and the toes on his right foot from frostbite, and a crippling arthritic condition caused by his long confinement, following his abduction by a Chinese warlord, in a cage where he could neither stand nor recline. (His escape from captivity, abetted by one of the warlord's concubines, including his trek across a treacherous mountain pass, considered impassable in winter, was part of both public record and national legend, and although it was never filmed, a screenplay based on these exploits was developed with serious consideration given to Josef von Sternberg as its director and Marlene Dietrich in the role of the concubine.)

These exploits were in the minds of most as the Rector arose painfully from his chair. As he approached the lectern, leaning on his cane with one hand and on the arm of the Chancellor with the other, the audience applauded vigorously.

Although in the privacy of his home or in the field he often wore the traditional garb of the peoples he studied—a gakti or a Mongolian dal—he was now dressed in his usual lecture-hall attire, and his double-breasted, knee-length frock coat, loose tie, and stiff collar along with his bushy steel-gray moustache gave him the appearance of a previous generation, as if he were there to represent the past rather than to inaugurate the future. He spread his notes out before him, and without any introduction or expression of gratitude or deference, as if what he had to say was too important to bear the burden of formality, he began:

"Absolutely no one today seriously doubts the scientific validity of the concept of race. We, the distinguished gentlemen sitting behind me; you, the audience before me; along with the porter at the door and the scullery maid in the kitchen, all recognize and understand it as soon as we walk into the streets of this great modern city. It is, of course, fundamental to the taxonomy of humanity and derives from one of the foundational texts of the natural sciences, the

Systema naturae of Carolus Linnaeus himself. There he classified the four races of man that we still identify to this day: *Europeus, Asiaticus, Afer, Americanus*. His disciple Blumenbach, in his *De generis humani varietate nativa*, provided us with the more familiar nomenclature: Caucasian, Mongolian, Ethiopian, and American. He also took the liberty of adding a fifth category, Malayan, which I view—as many of my colleagues in the audience know—as an unnecessary and misguided aberration."

He paused for a moment, as if awaiting for the majority of the audience to endorse this observation with assenting nods and murmurs, before resuming: "Of course, all taxonomies—the human as well as the animal—are subject to expansion and variation as genera and subspecies are discovered and identified, and in Europe alone, we now encounter such diverse subtypes of the Caucasian as the Nordic, the Falish, the Mediterranean, the Alpine, the Dinaric, the East Baltic, with perhaps more to come. In addition, we have experienced spirited debate concerning the relative importance of the cranium over the corpus and vice versa, the phenotype over the genotype, physiology over psychology, and so forth. But none of this as yet has negated the essential racial classification first proposed in 1758. Still, what has been missing, until now, has been a rigorous scientific delineation—objective and empirical—to help us establish once and for all the physical identity and boundaries of each of the core races. I say until now, for that is exactly what these expeditionary teams will be setting out to achieve. Early tomorrow morning they will embark on long and perilous journeys of discovery from which all those involved in the study of humanity—indeed, all those concerned about the progression of scientific knowledge itself—will benefit and be forever grateful!"

At these words, the audience arose as one to applaud, and hearty cheers erupted from the teams in the front rows. When they were all again seated, the Rector began to describe the arduous search undertaken to locate the ideal sites for each of the three studies. These would be small communities with roots in prehistory, yet far from migratory or trade patterns, isolated enough to be largely dependent on parochial economies and technologies, and relatively free from what the Rector termed "demographic and cultural adulteration." Hundreds of potential sites were proposed and rejected, and although, as the Rector explained, "Nothing can be perfect in this ancient, evolving world of ours," three where "racial hegemony had remained largely undisturbed for centuries" were finally chosen: A village in the mountains of Jämtland near the Norway-Sweden border, an enclave of the Damara tribe surrounded by the Namibian desert and a pestiferous forest to the south, and a Yunnan valley as remote as Shangri-La where families of Yin peasants had lived undisturbed for centuries. Regretting that funding could not be found to support a fourth expedition to the Americas, the Rector predicted that, "Once the value of these our current endeavors is appreciated, financial support will certainly be forthcoming for a fourth expedition and the completion of our task."

But in the meantime, all resources had been devoted to the training and support of the current teams, who were equipped with the latest and most precise instruments (although the Rector failed to mention that the cost of their kits had been underwritten by the manufacturer himself who hoped to see a surge in demand for his products should the outcome of the expeditions lead to the wide applications anticipated by its sponsors).

"Tools like these," said the Rector, holding aloft a small caliper, "many of them custom-made and calibrated for this specific mission," and, perhaps for the first time in human history, this humble instrument was the object of a standing ovation.

"A total of twenty-five bone, sliding, and skinfold calipers in each kit," he continued, even before the applause ended, "along with anthropometers and head-squares, all required for the minimum of eighty-five measurements—from the length and height of the skull, to the width and length of the digits to the thickness of the nose, base, middle, septum—applied to every man, woman, and child in the set. And that's only the beginning. Ratios—forearm to humerus, say, height to waist, and so forth—may be as distinctive and revelatory as the lengths and widths themselves. The possible permutations are, of course, endless, but once the process is complete we will have not only a clear and standard, data-driven identity for these three core races, but also, ideally, we will have reduced the data for each to a single mathematical formula as distinct, as descriptive, and as absolute as skin color or the thickness of hair. A final determinative starting point," he declared, "for the clarification of racial identity!"

These results were destined to be both standard and definitive, but the Rector cautioned his audience, reminding them that the results were also intended to be only descriptive, and no more. "We leave," he suggested, "to the ethnographers, the philosophers, and the politicians the task of creating social and cultural values from these findings, of providing guidance and formulating policies. Although there is little doubt that the immutability of somatological characteristics have equally immutable psychological and social properties, leading, if properly understood, organized, and controlled, to more stable and workable social structures, it is not our intention to qualify our investigations; nevertheless, for the record, I would like to confirm that my own decidedly dolichocephalic skull has a pronounced Nordic cranial index of 75!"

This comment at first elicited only a few scattered pockets of laughter, as if most in his audience were uncertain that the Rector, who rarely injected humor into his lectures, was actually joking here.

"Of course, I'm only stating the obvious," he added, and reassuring his audience with a wide grin that he was indeed being clever, he then needed to pause for a moment until the now generalized laughter had subsided.

"But we will not be ignoring the social and cultural status of the populations under controlled study," and the Rector mentioned how the teams were trained in survey and interrogatory techniques free of narrative and other biases, to elicit not only genealogical profiles and histories—lineage and kinship ties necessary for the interpretation of the metrical data—but also insights into rituals and spiritual beliefs, family and domestic practices, dietary and hygienic habits. "This supplementary material," he explained, "would be reviewed and edited to comprise the addenda of the intended three volumes, or perhaps a fourth volume, of *Mankind: The Racial Topography*."

He paused, and then, with emphasis, repeated, "Yes, *Mankind*! A year from today, our teams will have returned home—tanned, in good health, and intact, I'm sure—with their data sets, supplemented by a wealth of field notes and photographic evidence, along with specimens and artifacts for our laboratories and museums." They would then, he said, be joined by additional teams of scientists and researchers, many of them skilled in mathematics and statistics, who would evaluate, correlate (supplying, on occasion, fresh perspectives and new insights), and finally prepare the material for publication.

"Yes, *Mankind: The Racial Topography*!" he again repeated. "A work destined to become as seminal to the human sciences as

Newton's *Principia* was to physics and Copernicus's *De revolutionibus orbium coelestium* was to astronomy."

"And just as from those works huge changes in scientific thought, intellectual progress, and civilization itself erupted," he declared, "we would expect the expeditions we undertake tomorrow to lead to an era of further exploration and discovery, new applications and departures that will, in turn, lead to expanded departments and divisions of our great institutions, and perhaps the establishment of new institutions themselves. We are, as it were, building on a foundation set by our predecessors some two hundred years ago, or, better yet, nourishing the roots of a venerable oak tree that will grow and flourish for years to come!" And then as he flattened his palms and stretched and lifted his arms, the teams in the front rows arose as if they were puppets on a string, turning to face their audience. "And it is these trained professionals who are destined to become the teachers and mentors of succeeding generations, the scientists and technicians who will determine our future."

The teams bowed to acknowledge the applause, and after the Rector lowered his arms and they were again seated, he leaned on the podium and stared silently and intently forward, peering, it seemed, directly into the future. "And just as these teams are setting out to define and expand our vocabulary and fortify the epistemological foundation of our field, their insights and influence will extend into every corner of intellectual life. Moreover, there are innumerable social and economic applications for the knowledge we are seeking, and even now, at the dawn of this new era, professional and technical competence is increasingly in demand—and amply rewarded—in the medical, legal, educational, and political spheres. Doctors and hospital personnel, lawyers and judges, teachers and administrators, social workers and genealogical researchers all require expertise and training, not to mention the corporate and industrial partnerships that are even now being explored and sure to become realities."

He paused, and then as he came to his conclusion and straightened his posture, he seemed to gain an inch or two in height and the very width of his shoulders seemed to expand. "A new Age of Discovery is at hand, and we are here to observe and guide its development and participate in its material and intellectual fortunes. Just as during that first wave of global exploration, the Columbuses, the Cooks, the von Humboldts required cartographers to map and name the geography of newly found worlds down to the smallest inlet and stream if they were to exploit their knowledge, we are setting out tomorrow, along with these young adventurers, to chart the longitudes and latitudes of human difference, to define once and for all the true contours for the continents of race!"

As he approached this, the end of his address, the Rector had raised his voice gradually, and just as gradually his audience arose to its feet and began to applaud and cheer, eventually drowning out his final words and the obligatory salute to the current regime that ended most of the public presentations of the day.

The members of the three teams in the front rows then turned toward each other, shaking hands, hugging, and slapping one another on the back. When those behind saw this display of comradeship and affection, they broke out again in loud and enduring applause. The Rector, from his position behind the lectern, also applauded vigorously until he was finally led from the stage to the floor by the Chancellor, where they both disappeared into the crowd, which by then had surged forward to the front beneath the podium.

Once the cheering and applause finally subsided, the three teams filed into the adjacent dining hall, where they were joined by their faculty advisors and a select group of professors, government officials, family, and friends. There were many toasts, wine and beer flowed freely, and the ensuing party lasted until the early morning hours, although by then the members of the expeditions had long since departed since they would be leaving for each of their separate destinations shortly before sunrise.

A month later the war broke out, and all three expeditions were recalled. Unfortunately, none of the members of the Chinese team survived the mudslide that swept their bus off a mountain road into a remote valley. The two other teams returned intact, although one of the two women researchers, a member of the African group, died two weeks later from an unidentified degenerative disease, probably contracted while in the field.

ELEVATOR DOWN

They were alone in the elevator, and then he was gone, and she hardly realized what had happened to her as she slid to the floor, her back against the wall, and when it reached the top and shuddered to a halt, she fell forward among the broken bags of groceries. The doors opened and then slid shut, and as she descended alone, she began to think—appropriately enough, but perhaps also stimulated by the memories of the dreams now rising to the surface—of elevators.

Even before they had entered her dreams, she had been an observer, studying elevators not so much because of their utility and purposes—and she was well aware that without their technology, the powerful skyscrapers at the center of the cities she loved would never have been built—but because of the ornamentation architects so frequently lavished on them. Often she would wander into the lobbies of notable buildings to see how the design and even the materials—polychromatic marbles, glazed terracotta tiling, burnished brass, and polished chromium—from the great portals at the entryways and street level facades had been incorporated into the interior and concentrated there. At the core, almost always, were the elevator banks, and it was here that the building's design would often be replicated in miniature, and even embellished; the doors framed with fluted pillars and Corinthian capitals, foliate cornices and incised lintels, frescoed and mosaic-colored pediments, and their surfaces decorated with shields and cartouches, floral wreaths and botanical fretwork, geometric and abstract shapes in copper and varnished wood. Sometimes, animating the heart of the building and breathing life into it, were caryatids and gargoyles, mythic creatures and heraldic beasts, pantheons of gods and demigods, and the elongated Arte Moderne nudes, in high and low relief, covered with gilt or incised into the brass, but invariably absorbed into the architecture just as these styles had been absorbed into her own work as in layout after layout she repeated the languages of previous decades as if the ornamentation of Rockefeller Center or Chicago's Marquette Building had been infused into her own designs.

But now she was inside, stretched out on the floor of the elevator at the heart of her own apartment building, descending in a car as nondescript as a freight elevator, with its olive-gray Formica walls devoid of any decoration other than the license above the operating panel, which she vaguely recalled mandated an occupancy of no more than ten, and now that her cheek was against the floor, she wondered why the management had gone to the expense of decorating it with a simulated Oriental rug within whose pattern—now soaked by broken eggs and splattered milk—she could recognize only a few scattered elements.

"Acanthus," she thought, identifying the object woven into the pattern beneath her eye, and suddenly she pictured the sliding railed screens and elaborate grillwork in those turn-of-the-century buildings in lower Manhattan where her mother would take her for appointments with dentists and optometrists, and then shafts seemed to shoot upward from the botanical patterns in this ornate rug, growing into cast-iron garlands of palmetto and laurel, vines sprouting anthemion and fleur-de-lis, coiling into waves, scrolls, and trefoils, draped with festoons and tassels. For some reason, she recalled from architectural school a phrase of Louis Sullivan's: "plastic, mobile and florescent phases culminating in foliates and efflorescence," but she noticed that these fluid, growing shafts were culminating, rather, in stake-like sheaves of arrows and spears, razor-sharp at the points, and when the elevator seemed to shudder again and jolt to a stop for a moment, she thought she heard chains and cogs clanking and vibrating, and the exuberant wrought-iron filigree now whirled and tightened around her, narrowing into a cage like one of those ancient pneumatic lifts descending by jolts and starts down the center of a spiral staircase in some shabby European hotel.

(Of course, the elevator had neither stopped nor even shuddered in transit, and there were no chains or cogs to rattle, but she had spent a year studying architecture not because of any interest in engineering or mechanics but because of her fascination with architectural detailing, and now as Art Director for a regional travel and leisure monthly, she neither knew nor cared that she was currently

moving at a constant speed of 1.6 meters per second in a car suspended not from chains but steel ropes of single tensile wire, equal
lay construction, driven with minimal vibration and friction between guide rails of cold-drawn 370 N/mm   grade steel by an Otis
electric traction motor, worm and worm gear machined in one
piece, operating quietly and smoothly at 1,500 rpms.)

She tried to escape from the twisting, rattling cage by rising, and
the failed effort was enough to release her from the gratings and
iron foliage which disappeared and were replaced by images from
one recurring dream after another in such rapid succession that they
seemed almost to blend together, and even though she was now going down, she thought momentarily that she was rising, since her
dreams usually began with an elevator's ascent and occasionally
even carried her laterally through vast structures that expanded over
wide stretches of countryside, which she often could see, as if the
walls of the passenger car had suddenly become transparent and the
horizontal shafts through which she was traveling were enclosed in
glass. Near the end of her dreams there would sometimes be a descent, usually on a return journey from somewhere, but never that
precipitous and terrifying freefall that abruptly ended the dreams of
so many others, for rather than developing into fearful nightmares,
these dreams of hers seemed to serve as fissures into other worlds
of experience, premonitory and Delphic, and since they often trav-
ersed recognizable spaces in recurring sequences, they became for
her more like mysteries that had been told many times over, with
new elaborations and turns each time, yet each time seemingly
drawing closer to an inevitable end.

Usually she had been waiting in the lobby or first floor of an
apartment building or a department store or a large institutional
complex—government offices or a hospital ward—or a dormitory
or a parking garage, and since others had preceded her and she had
been waiting for some time, she entered the elevator without hesitation and sometimes with impatience, but always casually, with
some degree of curiosity and without fear, although once inside she
had no idea where she would be going or, in fact, that she wanted
to go anywhere at all.

Sometimes the doors opened onto the upper regions of a department store with aisle upon aisle of merchandise stretched out before
her—cookware and cosmetics and fabrics of every color and tex-
ture, stacked in great piles reaching to the ceiling—and each aisle

often spiraled into a maze, sometimes leading her to the center of a mall overlooking a precipitous atrium that circled, level after level, up into the shadows or so deeply down that she could see nothing more than a profound darkness beneath her. Sometimes she would complete several circuits around the atrium—one direction leading up, the other down—until she encountered another elevator bank, which often carried her into subterranean corridors, past steaming boilers and engine rooms onto a subway platform where she would enter crowded trains, eventually exiting some distance away, into urban zones of dark warehouse lofts and loading platforms and dim sputtering lights, vaguely reminiscent of the old West Side on the banks of the Hudson or Fulton Market at night, leaving her with little confidence that she would find a bus or a cab that would bring her any closer to her destination or back from where she had come or somewhere close to home now that night was falling.

Or rather than into a subway tunnel, she would descend into a cavernous train station—Grand Central or Union, but larger— where she would arrive just in time to catch her overnight connection whose destination she thought she knew but never for certain; or into an airport with long, sinuous galleries of souvenir shops and food courts and newsstands, all rarely leading to her gate but sometimes out onto the tarmac itself where she would run to board her plane; or even back down into the lower level of the parking garage where she would search for her car among countless aisles of other cars, to continue her journey onward.

Or sometimes the elevators would open onto a hospital waiting room where none of the doctors or nurses would acknowledge her presence, or onto the upper floor of a high-rise college dormitory, where her fellow students, sitting in the landing, playing bridge, were no more aware of her existence than were the doctors and nurses, and there she would wander the circular hallways going from one door to the next in search of her room. Or after a long sideways traversal, the elevator would stop in the attic of one of those monstrous sprawling structures, where she would walk up to the roof overlooking river valleys and waterfalls and mountain ranges and other panoramas that she found calming, although she was often troubled by her inability to find her way back to the elevators and to the salons and reception halls inside with their pink marble colonnades, crystalline chandeliers, ormolu moldings, gilded cupids and satyrs, inlaid and lacquered tables and buffets crowded with porcelain figurines and vases filled with roses, tulips, and white chrysanthemums. Or was it instead the nave of a baroque chapel with altars, rather than tables, surrounded not by classical demigods but angels and saints, shimmering in the light dyed by the stained glass?

The last time she'd entered an elevator in a dream—and this was the dream that now lingered the longest—it lifted her into an enclosed tubular corridor that encircled an atrium, like the ones at the center of the malls, although not nearly as wide, but narrow enough for her to see into the corridors across from her through the elongated portholes that extended the length of every level, and through the glass she could clearly see the faces of others who, like her, were pressing forward, all in the same direction, and like her, all wearing such similar gray tunics and pants that they appeared to be in uniform, and although she recognized many of them as they circled across from her, none seemed to hear her when she called out their names, and by the time she called again, they were gone.

The last fragment of the dream faded, and she saw only the acanthus leaf woven into the rug just beneath her eye, and then that, too, disappeared, gradually obscured by the blood seeping around her cheek and into the rug beneath her, and when she looked up, she saw that the wrought-iron grating had grown around her again, althhough this time it was bare of wreaths and scrolls and foliated ironwork, consisting only of a few bars, sparse and wavering, but still topped by the sheaves of sharpened spears and arrows she had seen so many years before on a grill fronting an elevator bank somewhere in lower Manhattan, and just as she was losing consciousness, the doors slid open, and she suspected that they were opening for her not onto the lobby of her apartment building, but onto a place that would be as enigmatic and unanticipated yet as much of a familiar mystery as any she had experienced before in her dreams.

THE AUDIT

A udit. The very word conjured for Henry Probst images of ledgers, balance sheets, statement, printouts, and battalions of pale-faced men hunched over calculators, pecking away at the keys. But Henry Probst was only an assistant clinic coordinator, and since when, he wanted to know, were assistant clinic coordinators audited? Banks were audited, multinational corporations were audited, mafia dons were audited, Dr. Finkel, head of surgery was audited, and Dr. Finkel's lawyer, too. But an assistant clinic coordinator whose salary was within hailing distance of the poverty level? Moreover, he had served time in the Emergency Room, and that alone should have counted for something!

Of course, he had been warned—by Mrs. Lipton, who worked across the aisle in G.I. Oncology and who often took a motherly interest in his affairs. "I warned you," she reminded him when informed of his upcoming audit. "I predicted what would happen if you went to one of them cheap television tax preparers. But did you listen? No! Smart guy!"

He tried to explain to her that he'd had no other choice. Ordinarily, on the first Saturday in April, he would have arranged his W-2 slip, two copies of the short corm, and a scratch pad on top of his desk, along with a few sharpened pencils, and a fountain pen. He would have read the relevant instructions twice, filled out one of the forms in pencil, and after double- and triple- checking the accuracy of his computations on his handheld calculator, he would have switched to his fountain pen and transcribed the required data in the allotted spaces, remembering always to staple his W-2 slip to the return and to sign at the bottom. No erasures, no itemized deductions, no extraneous schedules; nothing missing, nothing illegible. Everything neat and simple so that his return would slide through their computers without a wrinkle.

But this past year, there had been complications. No longer was his income composed solely of checks with such and such a percentile withheld for taxes, money he would never see nor ever expected to spend. This year he had received a considerable dividend from a trust established by his grandfather. He had begun to collect rental fees on the use of his van. He had earned a special bonus from the hospital director for working weekends in the ER. All this and more came to him in checks untouched by any third party, quickly converted into cash by tellers who counted the fresh bills directly into his hand—hard currency to be exchanged *in toto* for goods and services—and he was not about to relinquish these hard-earned dollars without a fight!

So, he had followed the advice of the man on the television—the man in the three-piece suit and steel-rimmed glasses, sitting on the edge of his desk in an executive suite overlooking the city; the man whose complexion remained gray no matter how often Henry fiddled with the color control—and he arranged an appointment with a confident voice that assured him he was making the right move.

The voice so impressed Henry that he thought for a moment he had actually been speaking with the man on the television, and on the appointed day, he put on his only suit, shined his shoes, and purchased a vinyl briefcase for his financial records. But when he arrived for his tax consultation, there was no one resembling an executive there to greet him. Nor did a receptionist direct him to an office suite overlooking the city. Instead, he found himself inside a rented storefront, its walls decorated with peeling campaign posters, an assortment of mismatched chairs positioned haphazardly around a pair of fiberboard coffee tables. The room's only occupant, sitting behind a battered desk within a semicircle of filing cabinets, was a young girl, who pushed aside her desktop computer when he entered and motioned him forward.

She introduced herself as Sherri, a name that hardly inspired confidence, and her first questions about his financial condition embarrassed Henry as much as if she had been a pretty medical technician inquiring after his family's history of venereal disease. But despite her youth, her professional manner gradually overcame his uncertainty. She explained the difference between "credits" and "deductions" and between "ordinary" and "necessary" income, and she sprinkled her commentary liberally with such terms as "equity," "fair market value," "exclusions," and "inclusions." Soon, they had drawn so closely together that their foreheads were almost touching, and they began to giggle—furtively, like two children playing at doctor and nurse—over potential deductions. By the end of the conference, she had assured Henry of a refund, despite his additional income, and Henry had asked to see her again. She declined his offer, since the man on television frowned on open fraternization with clients, but she promised to accompany him should he ever be summoned for an audit.

***

She was as good as her word, and despite his anxiety about the audit, Henry was pleased to see her again, perched stiffly on a stiff-backed chair, her hands folded neatly into the lap of her gray pleated skirt. "Please be seated," said the auditor, standing behind his desk, and Henry crossed over the worn linoleum floor—scuffed by the shuffling feet of a thousand apprehensive taxpayers—to the oversized easy chair that had apparently been reserved for him. Unlike Sherri's, this chair seemed soft and reassuring, oddly out of place among the spare furnishings of the district tax office. Just before sitting down, however, he noticed that the white Naugahyde upholstery had been smudged and darkened by the oils and perspiration of its previous occupants, and when he eased into it, it felt unbalanced, liable to shift position with the least exertion in any direction. The armrests, too, were shaky and uncertain, as if supported by gears and levers that might be set in motion at the slightest touch.

As soon as Henry was settled, the auditor, still standing, opened a drawer in the file cabinet behind him. Since it was identical to the one into which Sherri had deposited a copy of his return, Henry wondered if it had been conveyed directly from her office, and then, noticing the startling resemblance between the two drab rooms, he was suddenly struck by the disquieting notion that he had been mysteriously transported back to the rented storefront, although here no dust curled up from beneath the baseboards, and instead of out-of-date campaign posters, framed portraits of the Founding Fathers hung on the walls. A color photograph of the current President accompanied them, although at a higher level, as if to provide him with a clear view of the top of the auditor's desk and the papers being examined there.

As the auditor flipped through the folders in the drawer, Henry turned slightly and nodded toward Sherri. She ignored him, continuing to stare forward, as inanimate as a large doll, her smile immobile, her eyes as unblinking as glass, her forehead as shiny as enameled porcelain. Her tawny hair, which before had flowed seductively about her shoulders, was now tied by a pair of scarlet ribbons into two pigtails, giving her the appearance of a schoolgirl, and upon looking down, Henry discovered, to his dismay, that she was wearing white bucks and bobby socks.

The auditor finally extracted a folder from the drawer, and just as he sat down opposite Henry, two additional tax agents, who had been waiting by the entrance like warders, marched over to Henry's chair, flanking it on both sides. "Who are they?" asked Henry, leaning slightly forward.

"There have been threats," replied the auditor, staring at him through the same steel-rimmed glasses worn by the gray-faced man on television, and as the pair of shadows hovered over him, Henry realized he had made a serious mistake in agreeing to come there.

They had given him the option of being examined at the district office or "in the field," and at first he had considered scheduling the audit for his apartment, distancing them from the security of their own territory. But since he was accustomed to smoking pot in the privacy of his living room, he was reluctant to invite the government into his home. Moreover, the auditor was sure to be an inhabitant of the suburbs and likely to suspect the dirt and disorder of Henry's apartment. He would naturally assume that Henry—who was, after all, being audited!—was trying to hide something beneath the cloak of poverty, that his secondhand furnishings were in reality antiques, that his tarnished tableware concealed sterling silver, and that within his piles of books and magazines were hidden considerable amounts of unreported income. On the other hand, he wondered if Sherri would have been as terrified as she now appeared had he been audited at home.

"And now, Mr. Probst, if you have no further questions," began the auditor, "we can proceed to your tax obligations for the past year," and with a rustle of papers, he removed Henry's return from the folder. "Am I correct in declaring that these are the forms Miss Harris prepared for you?" At the mention of her name, Sherri widened her smile into a grimace, her breathing ceased, and spots of moisture broke out on her forehead.

Having no desire to prolong the ordeal by inspecting the forms more closely, Henry nodded. "Yes," he said.

"Well, then, I'm sorry to say there appear to be irregularities here that require some explanation."

"Irregulateries?" replied Henry, aware at once that he had misplaced a syllable somewhere, but not daring to venture a correction.

"For instance," said the auditor, clicking on his reading lamp and spreading the forms out before him like a winning hand in a game of gin rummy, "you've taken an exclusion on the overtime pay you received for your work as an administrative resident in the Children's Clinic."

"That's right... I... we thought it was okay as a... what do you call it... specialized training toward a degree in hospital administration?"

"The Tax Court has determined that payments received by medical trainees to enable them to pursue studies may be excluded if the purpose of such payments is to further the trainee's education. Apparently, the Tax Court is in agreement with you."

"I'm glad to hear that. For a moment there I thought—"

"The Revenue Service, however, has not yet given any indication that this position is acceptable."

"Oh," said Henry, and after the auditor checked a blank box on his worksheet, he lowered his pencil to the following line.

"I see you itemized your medical expenses, the greater part of which is allocated for prescription drugs unreimbursed by your employer's insurance plan."

"That's right," said Henry, for once his voice carrying a measure of certainty; this time he was covered. "I have this chronic back condition," and after removing a packet of canceled checks from his vinyl briefcase, he nonchalantly dropped them on the desk blotter. "I've got receipts, too. I'm sure you'll find everything in order."

The auditor flipped through the checks as if counting a sheaf of bills. "I see they are all made payable to something called 'The Community Co-op.'"

"A local cooperative. My membership saves me a few dollars on groceries and pharmaceuticals."

"I assume that such savings are realized in the form of dividends."

"That's right."

Sherri groaned.

"Are you aware that patronage dividends attributed to the purchase of deductible items must be included in gross income to the extent of the amount received if paid in cash, or to the extent of fair market value if paid in merchandise or property?"

"Well, no… I…"

"Hmm," murmured the auditor, checking another box and proceeding to the next item. "You received an article of furniture, a Victorian settee, as compensation for rental of your van, property valued by your client at $300."

"No way! It's a piece of junk! I did him a favor by taking it off his hands. It's not worth more than ten bucks!"

"Whatever its worth, it certainly would have raised your net self-employment income—which you declared as $398—to over $400, thereby making you liable for the Social Security Self-Employment Tax."

"Well, yes, and that's why Sherri… Miss Harris thought it best not to—"

A choked, gurgling sound came from Sherri's throat, preventing him from continuing further.

"Do you mean to say you were aware of your obligation and willfully disregarded it?"

"No… I mean, when you phrase it like that—"

"Need I remind you that although ignorance of a regulation does not excuse noncompliance and is subject to suitable penalties, willful disregard of said regulation with intent to defraud, evade, or defeat the tax constitutes a felony under the criminal provisions?"

"I didn't willfully disregard anything! I must've been ignorant of it. I wasn't informed. That's it, ignorance. I didn't know!"

He checked another box. "You've chosen to take advantage of income averaging, yet included income received as an accumulation dividend from a trust, which is clearly ineligible."

"Ignorance. I didn't know!"

Another check. "You received a bonus from your employer, which you excluded as a gift, but which your employer deducted as an expense, thereby indicating its intent as compensation for services."

"I didn't know."

"You deducted a new set of tires for your van as a business expense, but since this represents a replacement component, adding materially to the value of the asset as well as prolonging its life, the adjusted basis of the old part should have been deducted as an abandonment loss and the cost of the new unit capitalized as part of the total basis of the asset!"

"I didn't know!"

"But this is intolerable!" exclaimed the auditor, flinging his pencil to the desk, and even though he had hardly progressed beyond the midpoint of his worksheet, he began to gather Henry's tax schedules together into a single pile. When he had evened out the edges to his satisfaction, he intertwined his fingers, placed his folded hands on top of the forms, and announced, "I'm afraid an adjustment is in order."

"An adjustment?"

The auditor turned toward Sherri, and with the smile of an indulgent father, he said, "Thank you, Miss Harris. We won't be requiring your services any longer. We appreciate your coming here today."

"You mean I can go?" asked Sherri, her voice parched and cracking as if she had just survived a trek across a vast desert.

"Yes, you can go. Unless, of course, you have something further to add."

Without another word, Sherri hurtled from her seat and fled from the tax office, her gray pleated skirt disappearing across the periphery of Henry's vision like a small, frightened animal scurrying across the floor.

Henry now felt more vulnerable than ever. Sherri had not provided much support, but she had, in part, shared his predicament, and as soon as she had vacated the room, the auditor turned his full attention on him, his thin, obliging smile reverting to the tight-lipped earnestness that had previously distinguished his features. "You mentioned something about an adjustment," said Henry, no longer able to endure in silence the auditor's formidable stare.

Instead of replying, the auditor slipped Henry's forms into their folder, and, leaning backwards, returned it to its place in the file cabinet. He then bent forward, momentarily disappearing from sight, and after pulling open a bottom drawer, he extracted from it a small apparatus, which he set on the blotter in front of him and clamped to the edge of the desk. Resembling a miniature vise, it consisted of a convex platform and, standing at opposite ends, two vertical planes that reminded Henry of bookends. Jutting from the centers of the planes were thick screws, both filed to a sharp point and directed toward one another like a pair of minatory fingers. Constructed of cast iron, the black machine gleamed under the light of the reading lamp as if it had been specially polished and oiled in expectation of Henry's arrival.

Two crank handles, apparently connected to a series of gears, projected upward from the platform, and as the auditor twirled the one to his right, the screws spun and glided forward. When their points met, the agents, who were still standing beside Henry's chair, grabbed the backrest, and, as if by a prearranged signal, pushed downward. Henry suddenly found himself staring at the ceiling, his chair now flat as a marble slab, his arms pinioned to his side. Lifting his head, he saw that his legs had been raised into the air, suspended there by stirrup-like devices dangling from above, and though the cleft of his thighs, he watched as the auditor again turned the crank, this time in the opposite direction.

As soon as the screws had receded a certain distance from each other, one of the agents exited through a side door, and when he returned, he was accompanied by Dr. Finkel, head of surgery at the hospital where Henry was employed.

After dropping his black bag on the chair previously occupied by Sherri, Dr. Finkel neatly draped his coat over the backrest. "I believe you two are acquainted," said the auditor.

Henry nodded toward him as best as he could in his prone position, but Dr. Finkel had already removed a white surgical gown from the bag and was too busy trying to secure it to his waist to acknowledge the greeting.

"A considerable tax deficiency has been determined against Dr. Finkel," explained the auditor, "and in lieu of a levy against his property, he occasionally provides us with services."

His response was obscured by the mask now over his face, and as Dr. Finkel snapped on his rubber gloves, the auditor added, "Dr. Finkel is one of our most skilled operatives, and you'll find the adjustment to be relatively painless, but nevertheless, I suggest you incline your head in the other direction for its duration."

Henry did as he was advised, and when he felt the drafty coolness of Dr. Finkel swabbing an antiseptic solution between his legs, he closed his eyes and tried to think of something else. As the auditor had promised, there was no pain when the doctor made his incision, for he was a skilled practitioner, capable of working lightly and swiftly. But the dull pressure of his probing fingers was extremely unpleasant to Henry—like having a thumb jammed down his throat—and soon he began to experience spasms in the area of his solar plexus and the taste of sour bile at the back of his tongue.

Finally, just as he was sure he could contain the spasms no longer and the contents of his stomach would come spewing forth, there was sudden remission, a deflation of sorts, as if a slight weight had been plucked from his body. Opening his eyes and raising his head, Henry observed Dr. Finkel cradling in one hand—and protecting it with the other—a small sphere the size of a walnut, perfectly smooth, as golden as the rind of an orange and as glistening wet as a newborn child.

Balancing it on his palm, the doctor conveyed it to the desk where he leaned his elbow on the blotter and, after centering the sphere within the vise-like apparatus, he nodded twice. The auditor again began to turn the crank to his right, first rapidly and then gradually decreasing its speed as the screws neared one another.

"Watch it!" snapped the doctor as the sharp black points pressed into the sphere's soft, malleable surface. "You'll puncture it!"

"I know what I'm doing," replied the auditor, now tightening a bolt that apparently held the screws in placed. "We trained for weeks with water-filled balloons."

When the auditor had finished, Dr. Finkel removed his hand, leaving the small golden ball suspended in the air, impaled on the points of the screws. "Rough or fine?" asked the surgeon, his mask now flapping around his neck.

"This is only a minor adjustment," said the auditor.

"Fine, then," and Dr. Finkel went to retrieve his black bag, extracting from it what appeared to be a square of sandpaper. After retying his mask, he returned to the desk and held the sandpaper poised above the apparatus. "Ready," he said.

The auditor arose, pressed his palm against the desk for leverage, grabbed the handle to his left, and began to crank it, fiercely. The screws and the sphere between them spun rapidly in place.

As the doctor cautiously lowered the sandpaper, he shifted his position, obscuring Henry's view of the operation. But when a shimmering spray of moist gold spurted into the air like a fountain, Henry dropped his head to the backrest and shut his eyes as tightly as he could.

It wasn't long before the whirring of the machine ceased, and the doctor was again twisting his fingers inside Henry. Once more he was almost overcome by a dull, warm nausea, and he feared that the procedure was about to be repeated. But this was only a minor adjustment, and the doctor quickly stitched him back up, leaving Henry's other "asset" (as he heard the auditor term it) untouched. The agents then released his arms and manipulated the chair back into its upright position. When Henry opened his eyes, he discovered that Dr. Finkel had gone, the apparatus had vanished, and all that remained of the thin, golden shower was a gleam here and there within the cracks of the desk's varnish and between the hairs of the auditor's wrist.

"Sign this," said the auditor, offering Henry a form and indicating with his pen a space marked with an X. "It certifies your consent to our assessment of your deficiency. No further adjustment unfavorable to you will be initiated, unless evidence of criminal fraud, malfeasance, collusion, concealment, or material misrepresentation manifests itself."

Henry signed the form and then struggled to rise, but the armrests he clutched for support proved unsteady, and he was unable to maneuver out of the chair. Sensing his difficulty, the pair of agents beside him lifted him to his feet, but rather than thanking them for their assistance, Henry pulled angrily at the cuffs of his sports coat, smoothing out the wrinkles they had caused.

"Would you like me to summon a cab?" asked the auditor. "We know you usually travel by bus, but if you're experiencing some discomfort..."

"I can look after myself," said Henry.

"I'd take it easy for a few days. There'll be some irritation, but it will pass in time. Dr. Finkel is a very skillful surgeon."

Henry refused to respond further, striding to the door and out with as much dignity as he could manage, ignoring the pain now settling between his legs. Disdaining the auditor's advice, and the continuing pain, he appeared at the hospital the following morning and worked the full day. Only Mrs. Lipton noticed he was limping, and when he passed Dr. Finkel in the hallway, he was gratified by the expression of surprise on the surgeon's face.

The pain eventually diminished and faded away. But sometimes late at night, during moments between waking and sleep, or during the day when the boredom of filing medical charts caused his mind to wander, he could again feel the raw soreness at his loins and remember the nausea from the doctor's probing fingers and wonder if the experience of the audit had been implanted so firmly into his being that it would linger there forever, to be transmitted from one generation to the next, without end.

MR. VESEY COMES TO WORK

Although he had died the previous morning, Mr. Vesey decided to go to work anyway. His wife, of course, tried to stop him. His company had been informed, she told him, friends and relatives had been advised, arrangements had already been made with the funeral home, and she offered all sorts of other plausible reasons as he was buttoning his shirt and knotting his tie. But it was Monday, and he was, after all, the Budget Officer for the Planning and Budget Department. Not only were they in the middle of their three-year planning cycle, but his fourth-quarter budget review was due that very same week. He might be late, but considering the circumstances, how could he possibly not go to work, he asked, as he grabbed his briefcase and hurried out the door to catch the 11:40 downtown.

It was a dank, overcast day, and the gray pallor of his skin and the shadows around his eyes drew little attention from the other passengers or from the pedestrians on the street as he left the station to walk the few remaining blocks to his office. Once he arrived, none of his coworkers on the ground floor took particular notice, since news of his death had not yet spread much beyond the Planning and Budget or Human Resources departments. But when he reached the eighth floor, many of his colleagues—as if drawn there by some magnetic premonition—stared at him from the thresholds of their cubicles as he passed. Vesey, of course, attributed the shock and surprise he saw on their faces to the lateness of his arrival. He prided himself on his punctuality, and if he were to be absent for even an hour, he always gave sufficient notice to his supervisor, Mr. Wilson. Understandably, then, he stopped on the way to his office to inform Wilson that he had finally arrived.

"Sorry, to be so late, boss," he said after first tapping on the open door and leaning forward into the room. "Something came up. But

I'll have that quarterly review on your desk before the end of the day," and he paused there for a moment, holding onto the doorknob for support, awaiting Wilson's reply.

Wilson, his eyes widening, was unable to respond other than with a brief nod and a weak smile. Vesey would have returned the smile, but since facial expressions had become difficult for him, he settled for a short, stiff bow.

Continuing down the corridor, he encountered Mrs. Richmond, the Office Manager, and after informing her that he was not to be disturbed, he unlocked the door to his office and closed it behind him. Mrs. Richmond watched him disappear into his office, and then, after staggering a few steps forward, she grabbed the top of a partition to regain her balance. Following several deep breaths, she continued onward, striding slowly and carefully into the restroom, where she promptly fainted, suffering a nasty bruise on her forehead when she collided with a sink on her way down to the floor.

Wilson, after studying the shaft of light slanting in from the corridor for several moments, rose from his desk, shut the door, and dialed Vesey's home number. Mrs. Vesey had called him personally late Sunday afternoon to inform him of her husband's sudden death, and now, before reporting this new development to upper management, he wanted to be absolutely certain he had all his facts in order.

"I know! I know!" replied Mrs. Vesey, a nervous tremor beneath her voice. "I did my best to stop him, but he just wouldn't take 'no' for an answer. Something about the fourth-quarter review."

"Yes, but he's dead, isn't he? Or has there been some sort of mistake or something?"

"There's been no mistake."

"But how can I... what can I tell my staff? I've already announced it to them, and I'm sure it's gone well beyond the eighth floor by now. In fact, I sent the bereavement notice down to the Print Shop first thing this morning. People need to know about the funeral. They'll want to pay their respects."

"Well, they'll simply have to make adjustments. God knows, I've had to. I've been calling everyone, telling them the funeral's been temporarily postponed, and I've tried to explain why. But how can I? I can't explain a thing! Fortunately, Simon Brothers has been very professional, very understanding. They seem to know about these things. God knows, I don't!"

The nervous tremor had turned into hiccups, and, realizing that there was no point in badgering the widow any further, Wilson again offered his condolences and hung up. But his hand remained on the receiver, and after raising it again to his ear, he dialed the Director of Human Resources.

Mrs. Abercrombie, in fact, was just then about to call him. Through some sort of corporate telepathy, Human Resources was usually instantly aware of any disturbances or unusual circumstances affecting the staff, and the department already had the incident under discussion. Given such short notice, however, they had not yet reached agreement on how to resolve or even to deal with the problem, and Abercrombie could provide little direction to Wilson, who was concerned about the impact of Vesey's appearance on his staff's morale. "Treat him normally," she advised after confirming what she already knew about the situation, "as if nothing unusual has happened. We'll get back to you as soon as possible."

"Sure you will," Wilson muttered into the dead receiver, and after locking his door, he spent the remainder of the afternoon sulking behind his desk, having no idea of what to do or even what his options might be.

Abercrombie, on the other hand, immediately called the Chief Operating Officer, Mr. Hildebrandt, who reported directly to the Chief Executive. After she briefed him about "the matter of Mr. Vesey," Hildebrandt informed her that the Chief Executive had just returned from lunch and would be available to discuss the alternatives. "But as you know," he said, "he likes things boiled down to their essentials and then acted upon at once. I'm reluctant to bring anything requiring a decision to his attention without a recommended course of action. Particularly today, just before his meeting with the Board. Exactly what, if anything, needs to be decided right now?"

Abercrombie reflected for a moment and then replied, "Well, over half the day's already gone, and there's a good chance there'll be no recurrence tomorrow. The Chief should be informed, of course, but I suppose the only decision we need to worry about today is whether to move forward with the bereavement notice, which is now ready for distribution."

"Fair enough," said Hildebrandt, and a few minutes later he had described the situation to the Chief Executive who, preoccupied with the spreadsheets his secretary had just laid in front of him, did not seem to share Hildebrandt's concern.

"Where is it now?" he asked. "This bereavement notice."

"In the Print Shop. Printed and ready to go. We've signed off on it for you, but, in view of the situation, you might want to take a look at it."

"Take a look at it? I never take a look at those things, do I?"

"Well, no, but considering the circumstances…"

"Circumstances?"

Hildebrandt was no longer certain that he was being followed closely, but he nevertheless continued down the same path. "Well, as I mentioned before, Vesey apparently was so concerned about submitting the fourth-quarter budget review under deadline, that, despite his condition, he came to work anyway."

"I would say that was very commendable of him, wouldn't you?"

"Yes, of course, but there are complications."

"Complications?" asked the Chief Executive, raising his eyebrows and looking at Hildebrandt directly for the first time.

Hildebrandt regretted having used a word that he knew his boss detested, but he persisted nevertheless. "The date of the funeral, for instance, given on the memo is Thursday, but that seems now to be unlikely. Moreover, his colleagues need to be informed of his passing, but if he continues to show up for work, that could cause considerable confusion. And beyond that there are the financial issues—the disposition of his life insurance, for instance, his pension payments, and the other benefits…"

"Isn't that why we have a Human Resources Department? To deal with such things?"

"Well, yes, but of course in his case standard procedures don't seem to apply, and—"

"Are you aware that I have to make a presentation before the Board in San Francisco tomorrow?"

"Certainly, I—"

"Do I have to do everything around here myself!"

"Absolutely not!" declared Hildebrandt, seeing that he had reached the limits of his boss's tolerance. "Just trying to keep you informed, sir," and he retreated toward the door, his eyes still on the Chief Executive, who had turned away to consult his day planner. "We'll take care of everything without further delay," he added as he exited, even though he could think of nothing better to do than to refer the matter back to Human Resources, which he promptly did.

Abercrombie, who had anticipated this outcome, had alerted her directors, and as soon as the problem was back in her hands, she assembled them in her office. Following the example of upper management, she focused their attention on a clearly defined, obtainable objective, deferring action on more complex issues only if the need should arise.

"Since the working day is almost complete," she began, "and we're not sure what tomorrow will bring, let's take this one step at a time. The Print Shop has been pressing us on the disposition of the bereavement notification. It's ready for distribution and they need to know what to do with it."

"Perhaps first we need to define the purpose of such a document," offered the Director of Development and Training, who also was experienced in long-range planning, "and see how it conforms to the present circumstances. What is it supposed to do, and does it meet the current requirements?"

"Good," said Abercrombie.

"I'll take a stab at that," said the Director of Staff Benefits. "I would say that it's intended to inform the staff of the death of an employee or an employee's close relative."

"...Which, as far as we can tell," said Abercrombie, "has occurred."

"And," added the Recruitment Director, "to inform fellow employees of the date and location of the funeral in case they want to attend or send flowers."

"But that information," said Abercrombie, "although available, is probably invalid since the funeral is likely to be postponed to a time as yet undetermined."

"And therefore," concluded Development and Training, "it would be inappropriate to distribute the memo in its current state, since it is inaccurate and incomplete, and thus incapable of fulfilling all of its intended functions."

All the directors concurred, agreeing that the Print Shop should destroy the current memo and that a new one should be prepared as soon as accurate information could be obtained. Abercrombie then adjourned the meeting and her directors filed out of her office, pleased that a consensus had been reached and action was being taken.

But beneath their sense of accomplishment, each of them also felt a lingering uneasiness. Their satisfaction, they all knew, was based on the expectation that Vesey would not reappear, that his presence there was some sort of natural aberration, like a snowstorm in May, unanticipated and disconcerting, but usually gone with the morning sunrise. They were all counting on a return to normalcy the next day, expecting that the incident would eventually be reduced to the stuff of corporate legend—like the job candidate who brought his mother to the interview or the box of hand grenades discovered in the mail clerk's locker—soon to become apocryphal, or, with the passing of time, completely forgotten.

But Vesey did return on Tuesday, shortly after one, wearing the same suit and tie from the previous day. Although he had worked late into Monday evening, he had neither the strength nor the energy then to complete the budget review to his satisfaction. Yet since with only a few more hours of effort, he could bring it up to his usual precise standards, he decided to postpone its delivery to Wilson—who had long since gone home, anyway. (In fact, several staff members were momentarily relieved by Vesey's arrival. Since no one had seen him leave the night before, there was some concern about what might be found in his office once the door was opened. Wilson waited until his lunch break before asking the Administrative Assistant, Ms. Bronsky—acting in place of Mrs. Richmond who had taken a day of administrative leave—to call the custodian. But just as he was unlocking the door, Ms. Bronsky fortunately looked up to see Vesey rounding the corner, and she quickly grabbed the custodian by the arm, pulling him safely into an empty cubicle.)

It took Vesey most of Tuesday afternoon to finish his review, and after checking the figures twice, he finally emerged to present the report to his boss. Wilson had, however, again locked himself in his office, and Vesey had to wait outside while he fumbled with the bolt. As soon as the door closed on them, the hallway filled with their fellow employees rushing towards the elevators. Although it was still a few minutes before five, they had all been waiting for just such an opportunity to escape the risk of a chance encounter with Vesey on their way out.

Also monitoring the corridor was Abercrombie, who, upon her arrival on the eighth floor to confer with Wilson, suddenly detoured into the coffee lounge when she saw Vesey waiting outside his boss's office. From there, she could watch the entrance to the elevator banks, and some minutes later, Vesey approached, looking very much like, thought Abercrombie as he walked towards her, an arthritic flamingo. When he pivoted towards the elevators, Abercrombie feared that he might fall forward on his face. But using his briefcase as a counterweight, he tottered back and forth and back again, and finally stabilized himself enough to press one of the buttons.

As soon as he was gone, Abercrombie hurried into Wilson's office, where she found him sprawled across his chair, a dazed look on his face as if he were awakening from a coma.

The pages of Vesey's budget report were spread out on his otherwise empty desk. Abercrombie sat down across from him.

"It seems to be very thorough," said Wilson, regaining his composure sufficiently to collect the pages and staple them together. "He always enjoyed doing these things."

"But he's finished with it, right?"

"Oh yes. Checked and rechecked, he said. I'll go through it tomorrow, but I'm sure everything's in place."

"And there's no more reason for him to return to work, right? You've told him that, of course, haven't you?"

"Well... not quite..."

"Not quite?" She paused, and then raising herself up, she leaned over the desk toward him. "What do you mean, 'not quite'?"

Wilson hesitated, finally admitting with some difficulty, "There's still the three-year plan."

"The three-year plan!" Abercrombie realized that the door was open, and she swung around to close it. Then, turning back to face him, trying to control her voice, she said, "You didn't say anything about that to him, did you? You couldn't have!"

"I didn't bring it up, he did. I couldn't very well lie to him. He knows as well as anyone that it's due in two weeks. It's always due right after the fourth-quarter budget review."

"But suppose he wants to do it?"

"Well, why shouldn't he? He knows the process backwards and forwards, and he's always done such a fine job on it, too. Don't you remember, the Chief Executive himself commented particularly on his work just last year."

"What are you trying to say?" asked Abercrombie, horrified.

"Well, you don't expect me to do the three-year plan, do you?"

"I expect you to act in a reasonably intelligent manner. I don't expect you to encourage him to come back to work day after day!"

"I didn't encourage him to do anything. He volunteered!"

"You could have said no!"

"What was I supposed to tell him? 'Why don't you go home and drop dead and get yourself buried like a proper cadaver?' Does he even know he's dead? Am I supposed to remind him of that? In fact, I haven't the slightest idea of what I'm supposed to say to him. I haven't the slightest idea what my legal obligations are or even what the potential liabilities might be! Certainly, Human Resources hasn't been of much help!"

"Whatever your legal obligations are or our potential liabilities might be," said Abercrombie, standing up and opening the door, "I know who will be responsible to senior management if he shows up again tomorrow to work on your three-year plan," and she left the office without giving Wilson the chance to reply and without, of course, any better idea than he had of what their legal obligations might be.

Vesey did come to work the following day—mid-morning, in fact, shortly after the rest of the staff had arrived. From his stride, he appeared to have lost much of the stiffness in his joints. His knees seemed loose, almost unhinged, and his body sagged forward with every step, as if the shifting of his weight alone were propelling him down the hall. Wilson, on his way to the coffee lounge, met him head-on, and although Vesey's greeting was pleasant enough, the expression on his face continued to be blank. The night before, Wilson had noticed a dark bluish redness around Vesey's fingernails as he pointed out certain expense overages and revenue shortfalls on the budget review. Now he saw the same purplish tinge at the tip of his nose and towards the lobes of his ears, and the faint marbling beneath his cheekbones would have convinced Wilson that Vesey had a drinking problem had he not known for sure that he was a teetotaler. A soft puffiness rounded the contours of his face, and his eyes bulged slightly outward, and although the whites were discolored with brown, as if spotted with maple syrup, there was a lively glint deep inside the pupils that Wilson could only interpret as an eagerness to begin his work on the three-year plan.

When he returned to his office, Wilson left the door conspicuously open. He would have preferred keeping it shut, but after having locked himself inside for two days, he realized that he would have to allow his staff some opportunity to express their concerns, even if he could provide neither explanations nor solutions.

As Wilson expected, Jacobson—who, despite his skill as a planning facilitator, often revealed a remarkable insensitivity to the feelings of others—was the first to storm into his office, slamming the door behind him.

"Get rid of him!" he declared. "Get rid of that stiff right now, or there'll be hell to pay!"

"Now listen, Harry," said Wilson calmly, accustomed to dealing with Jacobson's peremptory outbursts, "How about showing some consideration for the misfortunes of your colleague."

"Colleague? Who? That?"

"Harry! How can you be so insensitive? Charlie Vesey was your friend, wasn't he?"

"Him? Friend? No. Never!"

"Sure he was. A month ago you were playing racquetball with him twice a week."

"Is that it? You want me to challenge him to a game of racquetball? I don't think it would be much of a contest."

"No, that's not what I want. What I want is… is…" But Wilson didn't know what he wanted, and he never finished his sentence, listening silently for the most part as Jacobson continued to complain for another hour or so, wandering from Vesey to working conditions to the size of his salary to the lack of nearby parking.

Mrs. DeMarco, however, kept to the point. Her job as a Financial Systems Analyst required her to be exacting and punctilious, qualities which, at least in her case, translated into a certain squeamishness and an excessive concern for personal hygiene.

"I can smell him," she insisted, "and it's getting worse."

"That's nonsense," said Wilson. "I'm closer to him than you are, and there's nothing there."

"It's like a dark, sickly sweet aroma," she said. "The sweet smell of rot."

"Rather the sweet smell of aftershave lotion," said Wilson. "That's all that I've noticed," although he suspected that Vesey was applying heavier and heavier doses of it each day, and whenever Wilson approached the northern end of the corridor, he detected beneath the thickening perfumed aroma a stale, dusky odor, like that from a mildewed sock buried in a drawer of freshly laundered linen. Of course, he said nothing about this to DeMarco.

Ms. Riley had similar concerns, these resulting from Vesey's changing appearance. But Wilson knew that her father, to whom she had been very close, had died the previous month, and there was little he could say to alleviate her distress. "I'm afraid to get up to get a cup of coffee or a drink of water," she said, "I might run into him, you know, which I've done twice, and when I look up into that face with all the swelling and the bruises and the eyes, I can't help but think of Dad and what's happening... Oh, God!" and she began to whimper quietly into her handkerchief.

Mrs. Richmond, his Office Manager, also broke down into tears, but rather than an expression of sadness, her behavior approached hysteria, deriving not so much from any personal loss but from the profound belief that she was glimpsing the beginning of the end of all things. Earlier that year, Wilson had reprimanded her for distributing religious pamphlets on company property, and he wasn't surprised to hear her interpret Vesey's appearance there as a sign of the coming Apocalypse. "The dead rising from the grave," she said over and over again, "the dead rising..." and although Wilson pointed out that Vesey had never literally risen since he had not yet been buried, she continued to stammer on about locusts and scorpions and horned beasts and jasper thrones and fiery horsemen and the great day of the wrath of God. Finally, when she collapsed into what Wilson interpreted to be total incoherence, he sent her home.

Yet beyond these visceral reactions, none of Wilson's employees could articulate any valid reasons for Vesey's dismissal. He was guilty of neither theft nor violence nor insubordination nor any of a variety of other infractions that could have resulted in his immediate termination, and since Vesey spent most of his time processing numbers and data and had, in general, limited personal contact with others in the office, no one could claim that his behavior was any different from what it had always been. In fact, Vesey communicated primarily through internal email, and without his messages popping up regularly on their screens, most of his coworkers would never even have known of his existence (although those very same messages—no more sinister than a request for an invoice number or a cost estimate—had now become, at least according to De-Marco, as terrifying as a late night knock on the door from the Gestapo).

Still, the tension, discomfort, and anxiety provoked by Vesey's presence was clearly detrimental to the conduct of business. But, since Human Resources continued to be of no help whatsoever and

Abercrombie was now refusing to return his calls—apparently punishing him for failing to discourage Vesey from coming to work to complete the three-year plan—there was little Wilson could do to reassure his staff other than to say that once the plan was finished, Vesey would probably feel no further obligation to return to work. Unfortunately, the three-year plan was not due for another two weeks. Unless he delivers it to me early, thought Wilson. Now that's not such a bad idea, and after most of the department had left for the day, he walked over to Vesey's office and knocked on the door.

"Yes?" answered a voice, low and hollow as if it were coming from inside a cavern.

"Can you stop by before you go?" asked Wilson, leaving the door closed.

"Certainly," echoed the voice, and a few minutes later, Vesey appeared at the threshold of Wilson's office. Grasping the frame tightly, he leaned forward, seemingly reluctant to enter.

"Come in and have a seat," offered Wilson.

"I prefer not to," said Vesey, his voice still a deep rumble, his lips hardly moving as he spoke. "My knees lock and stiffen when I sit."

"Okay," replied Wilson. "Well, then… it's about the three-year plan. I've had to expedite the schedule. A new directive, direct from senior management. I'll need it by Friday."

Vesey tried to straighten up, but in doing so he began to sway backward and almost lost his balance before he grabbed the other side of the doorframe and steadied himself.

"Friday afternoon, that is," said Wilson. "Late Friday afternoon. By the end of the working day."

"I guess if I work on it through the night… and tomorrow night, too."

"If it wouldn't be too much of an imposition…"

"I don't think my wife will mind. She's moved out of the house, you know."

"I'm sorry."

"It's understandable. But I don't require much nowadays, and I can always send my laundry out."

"Of course, since you'll be working around the clock, Charlie, you can take off on Friday just as soon as you've finished, and then you'll have the weekend, and, yes, you should take the following week, too. You'll have deserved it."

"Hmmm," said Vesey, his murmur like the soft grating of tectonic plates moving somewhere inside him, and then, as he shoved away from the doorframe, he said, "I'd better get back to work then, if I'm to finish under the new deadline," and he lumbered back toward his office.

"The sooner you finish, the sooner you can take off," Wilson called down after him, and after slipping on his overcoat and grabbing his briefcase, he quickly left the building, the dark cloud that had shadowed his existence having lightened considerably for the first time in several days.

***

As soon as he arrived on Thursday morning, Wilson emailed his staff and the Financial Services Department, informing them that Vesey would be working day and night to complete the three-year plan, and the quicker they supplied him with the information he requested, the sooner he would be finished with his final tasks. He also assured Abercrombie by voicemail that their problem would be solved by Friday afternoon. "He seemed intent on finishing the plan as quickly as possible," he reported. "But he was so tired, too, he could barely stand up straight, and I'm convinced that once he's done, he'll finally want to call it quits, to rest in peace."

But despite the immediate response he received from both departments to his fact-gathering, Vesey did not finish by Friday afternoon, and Wilson waited anxiously, less and less capable of doing his own work as the hours passed. It wasn't until early evening that Vesey finally emerged and presented the completed plan to his boss.

It was bound in a polyethylene binder, and Wilson was pleased to see that Vesey had added, for the first time, an executive summary and an index. But at the same time, he was startled by Vesey's appearance. His face seemed to have become even more swollen, and although the purplish tinge at its extremities had largely disappeared, his entire complexion was now darkened by a greenish-yellowish pallor. The stale, penetrating odor that Wilson had sensed beneath the surface of Vesey's aftershave lotion was now filling his office with its stench, and when Vesey handed him the plan, Wilson noticed that two of his fingernails were missing.

"Looks great," said Wilson. "I really appreciate the extra time and effort you've put into this."

"I could go through it line by line if you'd like," he said, his voice now sounding as if it were coming from the bottom of a reservoir.

"I'm sure you've done your usual splendid job, Charlie. What's important now is that you get some rest. You've earned it, gone way beyond the call of duty. I was very serious when I recommended that you take off, and I won't be expecting to see you here next week."

"Oh, that would be impossible," said Vesey. "I have no time for that, no time at all."

"What do you mean?" asked Wilson, panic, like a sudden attack of nausea, surging into his throat. "You have to take some time off. Why, just look at yourself! You need a rest. A long one!"

"I'm sorry, but there's still far too much to do. Far too much. Just thinking about it almost suffocates me. It's piling up in there, you see, almost over my head, there in my office," and when he stretched his arm outward, pointing down the corridor, Wilson saw how loosely his jacket and shirt hung from him and how ill-fitting seemed the rest of his suit, bulging out in folds in some places, sagging limply elsewhere, as if the contours of his body had shifted beneath the fabric. "Piling up in there almost over my head."

"We'll bring someone in," said Wilson. "A temp. A consultant. But you just have to take some time off."

"No, no. Simply out of the question," said Vesey. "With all that work piling up in there? How could I ever rest knowing that there's so much to be done? No, impossible," and he turned to leave, his labors complete for at least that week.

"Don't go! Not yet!" cried Wilson, stepping out from behind his desk, reaching out to detain him. But at the last moment, his hand hovering over Vesey's shoulder, he halted and pulled it back.

"Simply impossible," said Vesey, continuing down the hall. "But I'll catch up. Eventually. Don't worry. Monday's a new day. See you then. Bright and early."

Wilson retreated backwards, collapsing heavily into his chair as if flung there by a violent wind. After a few moments of dazed reflection, he dialed Abercrombie's number, fully expecting to hear again only a recorded message. But she was just preparing to leave when the phone rang, and as soon as she heard the despair in Wilson's voice, she regretted having picked it up.

"Maybe he'll just lie down in his bed and stay there," she said, trying to reassure him after hearing about his latest encounter with Vesey. "Maybe he just won't get up at all on Monday morning."

"And maybe the sun won't come up either! Bright and early. That's what he said, and he meant it."

"Calm down. We can discuss all of this on Monday. But in the meantime, maybe we should shut him off, disconnect him. If he doesn't have access to the network, he won't be able to get any work done, and that might frustrate him enough to leave."

"He still has his typewriter and calculator, and he's very resourceful, you know. Besides, the last thing I want is to have him roaming around the halls, gathering information personally from the staff. You have no idea what kind of condition he's already in, and after two more days, who knows?"

"Look, it's too late to discuss this anymore tonight. Stick a note on his desk in case he comes in Monday morning, informing him that senior management is in strong agreement with you and that he needs to take the entire week off, if not more. Moreover, tell him that his three-year plan was just wonderful, the best ever. Maybe he's just looking for a little appreciation."

"It won't work."

"Whether it works or not, whether he comes in or not, the Chief will be returning from San Francisco Monday morning, and he'll be expecting a plan of action from us. I've already scheduled a meeting with my staff and the General Counsel for ten o'clock in my office. Join us there," and she hung up the phone.

Wilson followed her suggestion, and when he entered Vesey's office, he found it to be as uncluttered as ever. The tape dispenser was aligned neatly against the stapler, but at the center of the otherwise empty blotter was an open notebook with a to-do list that seemed to extend for pages. Wilson taped his memo to the desk, and then he hurried from the office as quickly as he had once retreated from the orchid house at the Botanical Gardens, desperate to escape the lingering heat, the steaming foliage, and the dense, fragrant air.

***

On Monday morning, Abercrombie had only to see the distracted look on Wilson's face to know that Vesey had again come to work.

"Bright and early," said Wilson. "Just like he promised."

"Have you seen him?"

"No. He arrived shortly after dawn. The security guard let him in."

"How did he look?"

"I don't know, but the security guard's taken the rest of the day off, and now Vesey's locked himself inside his office."

"You're sure he's still there?"

"He just sent me an email. He's working on a new spreadsheet for projecting overhead costs and he needed some numbers from me. Apparently, it's a project he's been considering for quite a while, and now that he's submitted the three-year plan so early, he'll have plenty of time to develop it."

"I'll get my staff together," said Abercrombie, and as Wilson followed her from the reception area into her office, she motioned him to sit on the thickly upholstered leather chair near the door. As her department directors arrived, each of them drew a chair toward Wilson until they were all sitting around him in a semicircle. At first, he didn't mind being so obviously the center of attention, but when they began directing questions at him, one right after the other as if he were a hostile witness in a criminal trial, Wilson objected. "Now just a minute," he said, his voice rising toward an edge. "I don't think I'm the problem here, am I?"

"No, no, of course not," said Abercrombie, "We just want to make sure we've got all of our facts together," and by the time the General Counsel arrived, they had begun to explore possible solutions.

"How about getting him on short-term disability? Just send him home?"

"But that would have to come from him or a physician, wouldn't it? It usually originates from the employee, right?"

"And we'd certainly need medical confirmation."

"We've got the death certificate, don't we? Isn't that enough?"

"He'd never agree," said Wilson. "As far as he's concerned, there's nothing wrong."

"But if the doctor insisted, for medical reasons…"

"I fail to see how coming to work could exacerbate his condition."

"Why not just fire him and be done with it!" said the Director of Development and Training.

"Fire him?" asked Wilson. "On what grounds? I wish all my staff worked as hard and with such dedication."

"How about his teamwork? That's part of his performance review, isn't it? From what you've been saying, your staff can hardly look at him, let alone work with him."

"Even if we wanted to terminate him, we couldn't just do it. We'd have to put him on a performance track, and that could take at least a month."

"He'd be a health hazard by then."

"That's grounds, isn't it?"

"We can't wait that long," said Abercrombie.

"How about for cause?"

"Like what?" asked Wilson. "Should I plant a controlled substance on him? Maybe a .38 in his desk."

"Perhaps he can be provoked…"

"Now just slow down," said the General Counsel, speaking for the first time. "Let's be careful where we're heading. I don't like what I'm hearing right now. In fact, we seem to be coming perilously close to a violation of Title 1 of the ADA."

"The Americans with Disabilities Act? What, are the dead a protected class?"

"I'll have to do some research, but the ADA does define the disabled person as anyone with an impairment that limits one or more major life activities."

"That would seem to cover Vesey."

"Moreover," continued the General Counsel, "I find this loose talk about firing him on the spot or provoking him into a terminable incident simply because his appearance is displeasing to some of Wilson's staff to be personally offensive."

"Displeasing!" exclaimed Wilson. "He's decomposing before our very eyes!"

"That sounds like a management problem to me," the General Counsel replied, "like your staff could use additional coaching or some sensitivity training."

"Fine," said Wilson. "Why don't you arrange the appropriate lunch-and-learn program, and I'll see that they all attend."

"Look, this is a serious situation," Abercrombie reminded them, "and we're getting absolutely nowhere. We've got to come up with something before—"

The telephone rang. "Excuse me," said Abercrombie, and after walking over to her desk and examining the display panel on the phone, she said, "And, speaking of the devil."

"Don't answer it!" exclaimed Staff Benefits, one of the younger members in the department.

Her fearful outburst caused Abercrombie to pause for a moment, but then shrugging her shoulders as if she had no choice, she lifted the receiver. They all watched in silence as she listened without comment, occasionally nodding and growing paler by the moment.

After hanging up the phone, she crossed slowly back toward the group and, stopping behind her chair, she said to Wilson, "I need to advise you that your friend, Mrs. Richmond, has been discussing the matter with our Chief Executive. Apparently she was waiting for him in his office when he returned from San Francisco this morning."

"Who's Mrs. Richmond?" asked the Staff Benefits.

"She's not my friend," said Wilson, his complexion now as pale as Abercrombie's. "She's my Office Manager. She's been very troubled by this whole affair, and there are, as you know, some religious issues with her. I've been trying to reason with her but…" and now he appealed to the entire group, "Well, you can see what I've been dealing with."

"Weren't there some rumors about her some years back?" asked the General Counsel. "If I recall correctly, it was with Vesey, wasn't it?"

"Those were only rumors," said Wilson. "Nothing to them, I'm sure."

"In any case," said Abercrombie, "I'm wanted upstairs. This meeting's adjourned. I'll keep you all informed," and as she headed toward the door, she nodded to the General Counsel, who accompanied her up to the Executive Suite.

Nobody knew how she could have slipped past the receptionist or his secretary unseen, but when the Chief Executive arrived—direct from his redeye flight out of San Francisco, suitcase still in hand—she was there waiting for him, almost lost in the far corner of the massive couch by his desk.

In fact, he didn't even see her until she rose and was rushing towards him. "Excuse me, excuse me," she was saying, but the Chief Executive hardly heard her as he retreated in surprise toward the door. Sensing his alarm, she stopped, and after excusing herself once more, she returned to the couch and dropped her head into her hands. The Chief Executive halted, too, and rather than alerting security, he dropped his valise by the door, walked over to Mrs. Richmond, offered her his handkerchief, and sat down beside her.

"You probably don't know me," she said, raising her head, her face filled with tears.

"Of course I do. You're Ms... Ms..."

"Mrs. Richmond," and as she wiped her eyes and cheeks, she identified herself further as the Office Manager for Planning and Budget.

"Oh?" replied the Chief Executive, now curious, although equally suspicious that he was not going to be pleased by what he was about to hear. "And tell me, Mrs. Richmond, why are you here in my office without an appointment? I'm sure you have a very good explanation."

"Yes, I do," she said. "It's Charlie.... I mean, Mr. Vesey."

"Vesey? ... Vesey? There was something about a bereavement notice, wasn't there?"

"I don't know. He's passed, though, that's for sure."

The Chief Executive's eyes widened, as if he'd suddenly noticed in plain sight an important document that had been missing for some time.

"Then it's true. He's dead yet he's still... still..."

"Oh, yes, he's still here," and after returning the handkerchief to him, she explained that just as she was settling into her cubicle early that morning, placing her handbag safely behind the electrical outlet beneath the desk, she looked over her shoulder to find Vesey staring down at her. "Those eyes. I swear to you they were black, like an animal's, and on fire, like carbuncles. And that voice, like from deep inside the pit of hell! ... He wanted some paper clips. I couldn't say a thing. I was so afraid he might touch me with those cold fingers of his. I could barely point to the right drawer, my hand was shaking so. He looked like he wanted to smile at me, but I don't think he could, and then when he bent over the cabinet, I thought I could hear his whole body creaking, or maybe it was just the sound of the drawer opening. But he moved so slowly and when he was walking away, I thought he must be in such pain..." She dropped her head back into her hands again as if to shield her sight from the memory.

"Well, yes," said the Chief Executive, "we're doing our very best to resolve the situation. I expect a solution to be in place within the next few hours. In fact…"

Mrs. Richmond again raised her head, now staring at him in disbelief. "My goodness," she said, "there's nothing you can do about it."

"Certainly, I don't suppose there's much we can do for Mr. Vesey personally," said the Chief Executive, somewhat surprised by the conviction of Mrs. Richmond's reply, "but there are steps that can be taken to improve the general ambience of the workplace. We have a very capable Human Resources Department, and I'm sure that they're on top of—"

"But you can warn them. That's what you can do, and that's what I'm here to tell you."

"Warn them? Who? About what?"

"'And the sea gave up the dead which were in it, and death and hell delivered up the dead which were in them.'"

"Now just one minute there, Mrs. Richmond. You're speaking of things now that neither I nor the company…"

"'… and they were judged every man according to their works.' Every man! They'll listen to you. You're an important person. A captain of industry! You can warn them so they'll know what's coming!"

"Really, Mrs. Richmond, there's simply nothing that I can do in that respect. We're simply a commercial enterprise, and it's not in my power…"

She stood up suddenly. "I should have known," she said, looking fiercely down at him. "'And the kings of the earth, and the great men, and the rich men, and the chief captains hid themselves in the dens and in the rocks of the mountains!'"

"Now, really, Mrs. Richmond, I don't think it's up to us to judge…"

"'Woe, woe, woe to the inhabitants of the earth!'" and then, as if suddenly realizing that she, too, was an inhabitant of the earth, she fell back into the corner of the couch, her general accusation now a personal lament, and just before her sobbing became uncontrollable, the Chief Executive heard her say, "'For her sins had reached unto heaven and God had remembered her iniquities, and she shall be utterly burned with fire for strong is the Lord God who judgeth her.'" Before long, her crying had degenerated into a low moan, and she was swaying back and forth on the couch, her arms wrapped around her knees.

***

"It sounds like she's come totally unhinged," said Abercrombie after the Chief Executive had finished describing his experience. "I remember Wilson telling me how troubled his staff had been about her 'religious extremism.' I suppose we could look into short-term disability for her."

"Do what you have to," said the Chief Executive, "but in the meantime, she's given us a glimpse into the future."

"The future?" asked Abercrombie, and she shared a bewildered look with Hildebrand and the General Counsel.

"You don't think," asked Hildebrandt, "that there might be some truth in what she's saying?"

"I can't speak for all of humanity, but I can certainly speak for this company, and that's the road we'll be traveling down if we don't deal with this matter at once."

"I'm sorry," said Abercrombie, "but I don't see how…"

"You don't? Do you have any idea of how much damage was done to Procter & Gamble when some lunatics publicized the fact that their logo was full of Satanic signs, proof that they'd made a pact with the devil? Well, just what do you think will happen to our stock price when Wall Street finds out we employ the living dead?"

"But they certainly can't blame the company for a fluke of nature that—"

"Fluke of nature? You mean like plagues of locusts and rivers of blood? Mrs. Richmond is a herald of things to come. But I have no intention of allowing this company to be presumed to be the launching pad for Armageddon!"

"Well, sir," said Abercrombie, "I'm here to report that we haven't been idle these last few days. I've had the whole department working on the situation, and here are the issues as we see them—"

"I don't give a damn how you see the issues! There's only one issue as far as I'm concerned, and here's what we're going to do about it," and after the General Counsel agreed that the proposed solution was both reasonable and legal, the Chief Executive ordered Abercrombie to implement it at once.

As soon as Abercrombie returned to her office, she called her staff together again. "I'll get right to the point," she said, once all her directors had gathered about her. "We're downsizing."

They all looked around at each other, momentarily wondering if the cuts were to be across the board and if some of them would be missing the following week. "But we were doing so well, weren't we?" asked the Director of Recruitment. "I thought we'd met all of our profit projections, and—"

"It's Planning and Budget. We're eliminating the entire Planning and Budget department."

"But then who…"

"Each major department will now be responsible for its own budget and its three-year plan. Since the review for this quarter is complete, we'll have three months for everyone to get used to the idea and a full year to train department heads on the planning process. The final drafting and consolidation of the plan, formerly the responsibility of Planning and Budget, will be outsourced."

"But when—"

"Today. Now."

"That's impossible. How—"

"Pull together the files from the merger. Model procedures for all action steps should be there. Most of it's boilerplate, and with a little tweaking, we should have everything we need. We'll spend the rest of the week preparing the necessary documentation and the severance schedules." She turned to her Assistant Director, who had been with her during the merger when several departments had been reduced by half. "Alert security. You know how unpredictable these things can be."

By the end of the day, Abercrombie and her directors had informed the staff of Planning and Budget of their dismissals and seen that all were escorted out of the building. With one exception, it was not as difficult as she had expected, and a few were even relieved to be released from the tension and the grim anxieties of the last few days. None complained about the severance package, even though some of the particulars were still undetermined, and most were grateful to have the services of a placement firm at their disposal for several months. Only Wilson, whom Abercrombie had always considered a solid and reliable manager, lost his composure, rising from his chair to declare that he had been betrayed. "Why I've been a team player throughout my professional career," he said, continuing his complaint, "and certainly every day of my life here. I've worked, you know that, long hours, often late into the night. In fact, I built this department practically from the ground up, hired the best and got the best out of them, too! We've produced for this company. We've done our jobs!" He insisted that he and his people had always placed corporate objectives first, often to the detriment of their personal lives, displaying loyalty and diligence at every staff level. "Why even Vesey... My God, look what Vesey..." He stopped in recognition of what he had just said, finally understanding that he and his staff had been overpowered by a calamitous chain of events far beyond their control, and the storm and fury on his face became as calm and as rigid as the surface of a deep mountain lake. Sinking back into his chair, he listened without further comment as Abercrombie described the arrangements she had been making for him and his staff.

Not until all the other members of Planning and Budget had left the building did Abercrombie pick up the phone and dial Vesey's extension. There was no answer, and rather than leave a message on his voicemail, she decided to deal with him directly, in his own office.

Even though the working day had not yet ended, the halls seemed unusually empty as she took the elevator to the eighth floor and turned north down the corridor. She knew how quickly such news circulates and the effect it has on morale, and she supposed that many employees had probably left early to digest the incident and confront their own fragility in the face of corporate reality. But as she walked down this long corridor, she began to sense her own vulnerability, and she wondered if she were making a terrible mistake, approaching Vesey unaccompanied and so late in the day on what appeared to be an empty and isolated corner of the building, to announce to him his dismissal from a job that, perhaps, had meant as much to him as life itself.

Upon reaching his door, she tilted her head close to it and asked in a quiet voice but loud enough for him to hear, "Mr. Vesey?" When there was no answer, she knocked, waited, and knocked again. After several moments more of silence, she took a deep breath and turned the knob. The door was locked, and after knocking once again, she returned to her office, frustrated that she had not yet completed her task, but relieved at not having to face Vesey whose condition, she understood, had deteriorated considerably since she had last seen him several days before, lurching toward the elevator banks.

As she was leaving the building herself, she stopped at

Operations to remind them to cancel the electronic keys of the affected staff. She also mentioned that should Vesey appear the next morning, he was to be directed immediately to Human Resources.

But he did not appear the following day, and when his office was opened by the custodian, it was, to everyone's relief, unoccupied. Abercrombie later learned that Vesey had called his wife as soon as he arrived home from his final day of work and informed her that he would not be returning to his job for some time, that he felt like he could benefit from a long, quiet rest. As soon as he hung up, Mrs. Vesey called the mortician, who had been waiting for just such a moment, and he accompanied her to the house where they found her husband lying in bed on top of the blanket, his arms crossed over his chest. He was still in the clothes he had worn to work, but another suit, his favorite one, was laid out beside him, dry-cleaned and pressed. He was buried in it early the next day, following a simple ceremony, with only a handful of friends and relatives in attendance.

Not until a few weeks later, when the offices of the former Planning and Budget Department were being dismantled and rewired for the use of Information Services, did Abercrombie remember that a bereavement notice, a courtesy extended to current employees and all deceased persons recently employed by the company, had not yet been distributed. Oh, well, she thought, anyone who cares probably already knows, and the notice was never drafted.

***

By late winter, Information Services had settled into the space. With the removal and rearrangement of most of the central cubicles, with the installation of new equipment—more printers, more copiers, more file banks—and the laying of new, brighter carpeting, few traces of the eighth floor's former occupant remained. Only the northernmost executive offices, along the corridor, were relatively untouched, although the one in the northern corner, once occupied by the now deceased Budget Officer, remained vacant until the new Director for Systems Analysis was hired.

He stayed with the company, however, for only a few months, until, finally, he was unable to tolerate the incessant flickering of the fluorescent lights overhead, the garbled voicemail messages, and the regular crashing of his computer terminal. Operations claimed that it was probably all a result of the rewiring, but he still insisted on being moved to another office. When management re-fused—"He's only been here a couple of months," complained his supervisor, "and already he's making unreasonable demands on our resources!"—he resigned, stating that he had never worked in a more unsettling environment. Although enclosed offices were at a premium, no one from the department volunteered to move into the northernmost office, and rather than risk the loss of another new executive—thereby fostering the spread of unpleasant rumors and the revival of disturbing memories—senior management decided to reserve the space for storage. This, however, was not an ideal solu-tion, since it was later discovered that all the data on the magnetic tapes being stored there had been systematically erased.

ABOUT THE AUTHOR

Weintraub's fiction, poetry, and essays have appeared in many literary journals and reviews—*The Massachusetts Review, The New Criterion, Prairie Schooner, Cream City Review,* and *Crab Orchard Review,* among others—as well as in regional and specialty publications such as *The Chicago Reader, Modern Philology,* and *Gastronomica.* Many of his pieces have been anthologized, and he has received awards for fiction and creative nonfiction from the Illinois Arts Council, the Barrington Arts Council, and Holy Names University. He has been an Around-the-Coyote poet and a StoneSong poet, and, as a member of the Dramatists Guild, he has had over fifty dramatic works produced throughout the USA and in Australia, New Zealand, India, and Germany. As a translator, he has introduced the Italian and Swiss horror writers, Nicola Lombardi and Davide Staffiero, to the English-speaking world, and his edition of Lombardi's *The Gypsy Spiders and Other Tales of Italian Horror* was published by the UK's Tartarus Press in 2021 ("Lovers of postwar narratives and surrealist horror won't want to miss this." - *Publishers Weekly*). In 2018, his annotated translation of Eugène Briffault's *Paris à table: 1846* was published by Oxford UP. He has a Ph.D. in English Literature from The University of Chicago. More at https://jweintraub.weebly.com.

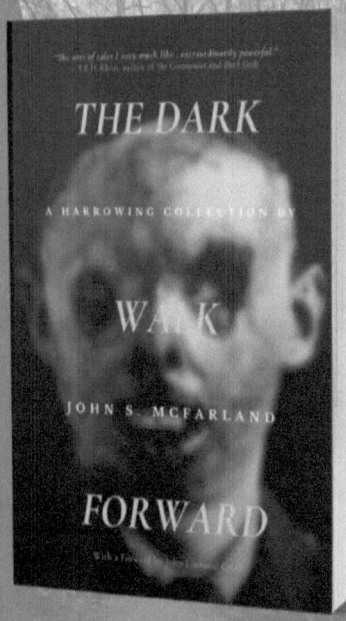

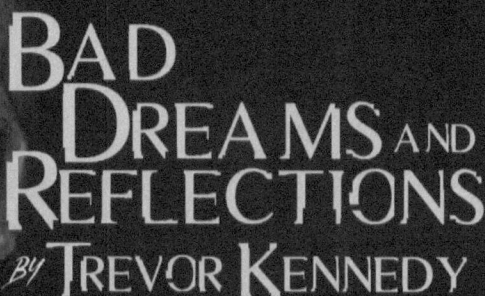

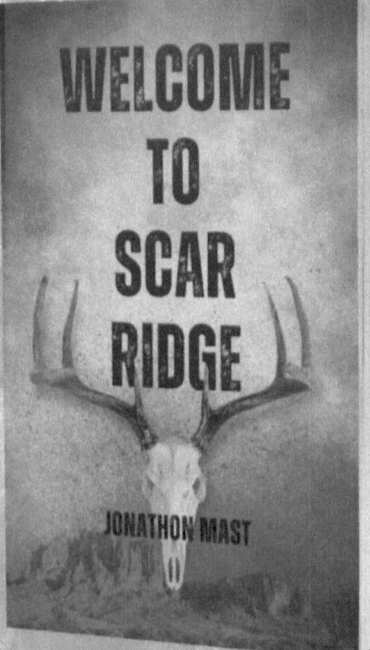